HBJ TREASURY OF LITERATURE

WOULDN'T YOU LIKE A DINOSAUR?

SENIOR AUTHORS
ROGER C. FARR
DOROTHY S. STRICKLAND

AUTHORS
RICHARD F. ABRAHAMSON
ELLEN BOOTH CHURCH
BARBARA BOWEN COULTER
MARGARET A. GALLEGO
JUDITH L. IRVIN
KAREN KUTIPER
JUNKO YOKOTA LEWIS
DONNA M. OGLE
TIMOTHY SHANAHAN
PATRICIA SMITH

SENIOR CONSULTANTS
BERNICE E. CULLINAN
W. DORSEY HAMMOND
ASA G. HILLIARD III

CONSULTANTS
ALONZO A. CRIM
ROLANDO R. HINOJOSA-SMITH
LEE BENNETT HOPKINS
ROBERT J. STERNBERG

 HARCOURT BRACE JOVANOVICH, INC.
Orlando Austin San Diego Chicago Dallas New York

Printed in the United States of America

ISBN 0-15-300420-7

1 2 3 4 5 6 7 8 9 10   048   96   95   94   93   92

Acknowledgments continue on page 310, which constitutes an extension of this copyright page.

Acknowledgments
For permission to reprint copyrighted material, grateful acknowledgment is made to the following sources:
Carolrhoda Books, Inc., Minneapolis, MN: Cover illustration by Kerry Argent from *Derek the Knitting Dinosaur* by Mary Blackwood. Illustration copyright 1987 by Kerry Argent.
Christopher Cerf Associates, Inc.: "On My Pond" by Sarah Durkee and Christopher Cerf from *Free to Be. . . A Family* by Marlo Thomas and Friends. Text copyright © 1987 by Splotched Animal Music and Jive Durkee Music. Published by Bantam Books in cooperation with the Free to Be Foundation, Inc., 1987.
Cobblehill Books, an affiliate of Dutton Children's Books, a division of Penguin Books USA Inc.: Cover photograph from *Never Kiss an Alligator* by Colleen Stanley Bare. Copyright © 1989 by Colleen Stanley Bare.
Dial Books for Young Readers, a division of Penguin Books USA Inc.: From *Snakey Riddles* by Katy Hall and Lisa Eisenberg, illustrated by Simms Taback. Text copyright © 1990 by Katy Hall and Lisa Eisenberg; illustrations copyright © 1990 by Simms Taback. Cover illustration by Steven Kellogg from *The Day the Goose Got Loose* by Reeve Lindbergh. Illustration copyright © 1990 by Steven Kellogg. *The Day Jimmy's Boa Ate the Wash* by Trinka Hakes Noble, illustrated by Steven Kellogg. Text copyright © 1980 by Trinka Hakes Noble; illustrations copyright © 1980 by Steven Kellogg.
Dutton Children's Books, a division of Penguin Books USA Inc.: "Under the Ground" from *Stories to Begin On* by Rhoda W. Bacmeister. Text copyright 1940 by E. P. Dutton, renewed © 1968 by Rhoda W. Bacmeister. Cover illustration by Elisa Kleven from *Abuela* by Arthur Dorros. Illustration copyright © 1991 by Elisa Kleven. From *It's an Armadillo!* by Bianca Lavies. Copyright © 1989 by Bianca Lavies.
Farrar, Straus & Giroux: Cover illustration from *Antarctica* by Helen Cowcher. Copyright © 1990 by Helen Cowcher.
Four Winds Press, an imprint of Macmillan Publishing Company: *The Goat in the Rug* by Charles Blood and Martin Link, illustrated by Nancy Winslow Parker. Text copyright © 1980 by Charles Blood and Martin Link; illustrations copyright © 1980 by Nancy Winslow Parker. Cover photograph by Ronald Goor from *Backyard Insects* by Millicent E. Selsam and Ronald Goor. Photograph © 1981 by Ronald Goor.
Greenwillow Books, a division of William Morrow & Company, Inc.: "My Creature" from *Rainy Rainy Saturday* by Jack Prelutsky, illustrated by Marylin Hafner. Text copyright © 1980 by Jack Prelutsky; illustration copyright © 1980 by Marylin Hafner.
GRM Associates, Inc., Agents for Children's Book Press: *Family Pictures* by Carmen Lomas Garza. Copyright © 1990 by Carmen Lomas Garza.
Harcourt Brace Jovanovich, Inc.: From *A Chinese Zoo: Fables and Proverbs* (Retitled: "Animal Tales") by Demi. Copyright © 1987 by Demi. "Fireflies" from *Dragon Kites and Dragonflies* by Demi. Copyright © 1986 by Demi. From *A Dinosaur Named After Me* by Bernard Most. Copyright © 1991 by Bernard Most.
HarperCollins Publishers: Cover illustration by Ned Delaney from *The Cactus Flower Bakery* by Harry Allard. Illustration copyright © 1991 by T. N. Delaney III. From *Ant Cities* by Arthur Dorros. Copyright © 1978 by Arthur Dorros. Cover illustration by Holly Keller from *Snakes Are Hunters* by Patricia Lauber. Illustration copyright © 1988 by Holly Keller. From *Four & Twenty Dinosaurs* by Bernard Most. Copyright © 1990 by Bernard Most. *The Chalk Doll* by Charlotte Pomerantz, illustrated by Frané Lessac. Text copyright © 1989 by Charlotte Pomerantz; illustrations copyright © 1989 by Frané Lessac. Published by J. B. Lippincott. "Instructions" from *Where the Sidewalk Ends* by Shel Silverstein. Copyright © 1974 by Evil Eye Music, Inc. "So Will I" from *River Winding* by Charlotte Zolotow. Text copyright © 1970 by Charlotte Zolotow.
Henson Associates, Inc.: Illustrations by Tom Cooke from *Free to Be. . . A Family* by Marlo Thomas and Friends. Illustrations copyright © 1987 by Henson Associates, Inc. Published by Bantam Books in cooperation with the Free to Be Foundation, Inc., 1987. Kermit the Frog is a trademark of Henson Associates, Inc.
Henry Holt and Company, Inc.: *The Empty Pot* by Demi. Copyright © 1990 by Demi.
Kane/Miller Book Publishers: *The Night of the Stars* by Douglas Gutiérrez and María Fernandez Oliver, translated by Carmen Diana Dearden. Originally published in Venezuela in Spanish under the title *La Noche de Las Estrellas* by Ediciones Ekaré-Banco del Libro, 1987. Published in America by Kane/Miller Book Publishers, 1988.
Harold Lavington and Jean Tibbles: "The Underworld" by Margaret Lavington.
Little, Brown and Company: *Awful Aardvark* by Mwalimu, illustrated by Adrienne Kennaway. Text copyright © 1989 by Peter Upton; illustrations copyright © 1989 by Adrienne Kennaway.
Lothrop, Lee & Shepard Books, a division of William Morrow & Company, Inc.: Cover illustration from *Sam Johnson and the Blue Ribbon Quilt* by Lisa Campbell Ernst. Copyright © 1983 by Lisa Campbell Ernst.
Gina Maccoby Literary Agency: "Ants" from *Yellow Butter Purple Jelly Red Jam Black Bread* by Mary Ann Hoberman. Text copyright © 1981 by Mary Ann Hoberman. Published by Viking Penguin.
Orchard Books, New York: Cover illustration from *Waiting for Billy* by Martin Jacka. Copyright © 1990 by Martin Jacka.
Philomel Books: *Thunder Cake* by Patricia Polacco. Copyright © 1990 by Patricia Polacco.
Picture Book Studio, Saxonville, MA: Cover illustration from *Rolli* by Koji Takihara. Copyright © 1988 by Neugebauer Press, Salzburg, Austria.

continued on page 310

Dear Reader,

Wouldn't you like a dinosaur? How about a silly snake or a friendly whale? You don't have to look too far to find them. They are all waiting for you inside this book.

As you turn the pages, your adventure will begin. You'll go from Jamaica to Russia and to many places in between. You will pick oranges with a family in Texas, smell a "thunder cake" baking, and spend some time inside an anthill.

<u>Wouldn't You Like a Dinosaur?</u> will make you laugh, think, and learn. We invite you to join us as we travel around the world through stories.

Sincerely,
The Authors

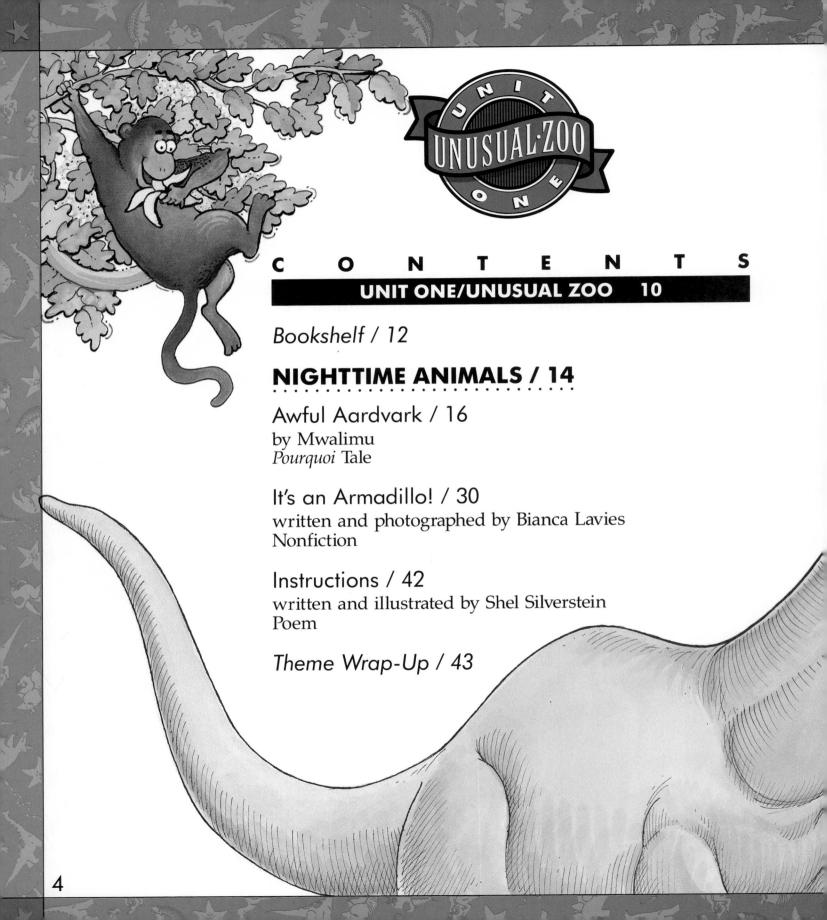

C O N T E N T S

UNIT ONE/UNUSUAL ZOO   10

4

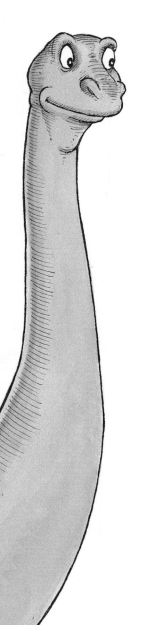

5

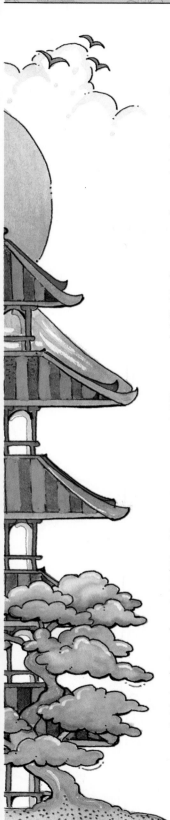

9

UNIT ONE

UNUSUAL·ZOO

The animals in this unusual zoo come from near and far, from today and yesterday. Some are real and some are made up. Artists such as Maurice Sendak use their imaginations to draw and write about unusual animals. What kinds of animals can you find in an unusual zoo? Turn the pages of this unit to find out.

11

BOOKSHELF

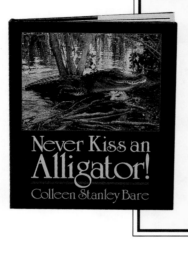

NEVER KISS AN ALLIGATOR!
BY COLLEEN STANLEY BARE

Alligators aren't for kissing or hugging. Find out why in this book full of alligator facts and pictures.
OUTSTANDING SCIENCE TRADE BOOK

HBJ LIBRARY BOOK

SNAKES ARE HUNTERS
BY PATRICIA LAUBER

Did you know that after one big meal, some snakes can go for months without eating again? Read more snake facts in this interesting book.   AWARD-WINNING AUTHOR

THE DAY THE GOOSE GOT LOOSE
BY REEVE LINDBERGH

A goose causes trouble in the barnyard when she escapes from her pen. Rhyming words and funny pictures make this book fun to read again and again.

WAITING FOR BILLY
BY MARTIN JACKA

This true story about a racehorse trainer, a dog, and a dolphin named Billy is set in Australia. The pictures show the warm friendship the characters share.

DEREK THE KNITTING DINOSAUR
BY MARY BLACKWOOD

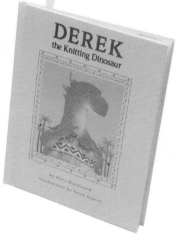

Derek wishes he were as fierce as his frightening dinosaur brothers. But his special talent for knitting comes in handy instead. When it gets very cold, even the fiercest dinosaur can use a warm sweater.

NIGHTTIME ANIMALS

Some animals sleep at night, just as you do. Other animals sleep during the day and are awake at night. Read the following stories and poem to find out about two unusual nighttime animals, Aardvark and an armadillo.

CONTENTS

15

NOTABLE TRADE
BOOK IN THE FIELD
OF SOCIAL STUDIES

AWFUL AARDVARK

Mwalimu and
Adrienne Kennaway

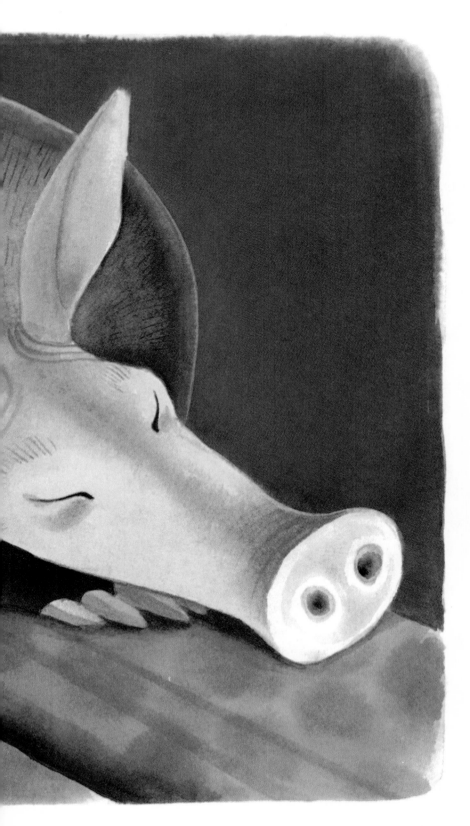

Aardvark was asleep in his favorite tree. The tree was old and dry, but it had a smooth branch where Aardvark would lie and rest his long nose.

And what a nose! His snoring was so loud that it kept Mongoose and all the other animals awake night after night. HHHRRR—ZZZZ! went Aardvark's nose.

"How awful," Mongoose yawned. "I wish he would keep quiet or go somewhere else."

Aardvark only stopped snoring when the sun came up. Then he clambered to the ground and set off to hunt for tasty grubs and crunchy beetles.

While Aardvark was hunting for breakfast, Mongoose had an idea. "I will just have to annoy him more than he annoys me," he decided.

First Mongoose had a meeting with the Monkeys.

Next he went to
see Lion.

Then he talked to
Rhinoceros.

19

That night, as usual, Aardvark climbed up to his branch in the tree and very soon he was snoring HHHRRR—ZZZZ!

Mongoose called into the darkness. The Monkeys came, and the tree shook as they chattered and screeched in the branches.

Aardvark woke up. "Stop making that noise," he shouted. But he soon went back to sleep and snored even more loudly than before. HHHRRR—ZZZZ!

Then Mongoose called out again. There was a low, rumbling growl as Lion came pad-pad-padding to the tree where Aardvark was snoring.

Stretching his legs and reaching high, Lion SCRAAATCHED the bark with his strong claws.

Aardvark woke up again. "Stop it! Go away!" he shouted. But soon he was snoring again, louder than ever. HHHRRR—ZZZZ!

Now Mongoose was very angry. He was so angry that his fur bristled. He sent out another call. The ground trembled as Rhinoceros came puff-puff-puffing to the tree. BUMP! Aardvark nearly fell off the branch when Rhinoceros pushed his fat bottom against the trunk.

"Go away! Leave me alone!" cried Aardvark. But still he did not stay awake for long. HHHRRR—ZZZZ!

"We need help," puffed Rhinoceros. "I'll tell you what we'll do."

Soon there came a munch-munch-munching sound from the roots of the tree.

Aardvark just kept on snoring.

Suddenly there was a loud snap and a crack. SNAP! went the roots. CRAAAAACK went the tree and it toppled over.

Aardvark bounced to the ground.

He picked himself up and glared at the other animals. "Who did that? Who pushed my tree over?" he demanded.

"Not me," said Lion.

"Not me," said Rhinoceros.

"Not us," said the Monkeys.

Aardvark snorted at Mongoose. "It was you."

"Not me," said Mongoose. "They did it." And he pointed at the broken roots.

Aardvark saw that the roots of the tree had been eaten away by hundreds of termites.

"I'm going to gobble you up," he threatened. He stuck out his long tongue and ate some of the termites. Yum-yum. He licked his lips. "I think I'll eat you all."

The termites hurried away with Aardvark following and eating as many as he could reach with his tongue.

In the morning the termites hid in the castles of sand and mud which they had built to protect themselves. But at night they still came out to eat the trees.

And from that time to this, Aardvark has slept during the day and eaten termites at night.

And Mongoose and the other animals sleep peacefully because they are no longer disturbed by Aardvark's awful snoring.

THINK IT OVER

1. Why does Aardvark stay awake at night now?

2. Why does Mongoose decide to stop Aardvark's snoring?

3. How would you have solved the problem of Aardvark's awful snoring?

WRITE

Imagine that you are Aardvark. Write a note to one of the animals in the story. Tell why you like to stay awake at night.

It's an Armadillo!

text and photographs by

BIANCA LAVIES

ALA NOTABLE
BOOK

OUTSTANDING
SCIENCE TRADE
BOOK

What has left these tracks in the sand? Something with four feet and a tail. You can see its footprints. You can see the groove made by its tail. Where did it go?

It went into its burrow underground. The burrow keeps it cool in summer and warm in winter.

During the day, it sleeps there in a nest. In the evening, it will leave the burrow.

Here it comes. It's an armadillo!

There are several kinds of armadillos in
the world. This one is called a nine-banded
armadillo. The bands look like stripes around
her middle. With her nose and claws, the
armadillo roots up leaves and twigs. She is
searching for food—beetles, grubs, and ant eggs.
Sometimes she also eats berries or juicy roots.

Every now and then the armadillo sits up on
her hind legs and listens. She cannot see very well,
but she can hear the sounds around her: a leaf
rustling, a twig breaking—even a camera clicking.

She also stops to sniff the air. Her keen
sense of smell makes up for her poor eyesight.
She can follow the trail of a cricket just by
sniffing. Now she smells fire ants.

The armadillo starts to dig. Her long claws make her an expert digger. Then she sniffs the hole she has dug, searching for ant eggs. Ants walk along her nose. They try to bite her, but they cannot pierce her tough, leathery covering. This covering is called a carapace, and it protects her body like armor. *Armadillo* is a Spanish word meaning "little armored one." But the armadillo does have some soft spots—the skin on her belly, the skin between her bands, and the tip of her nose, for instance.

The armadillo's long, sticky tongue flicks in and out, in and out, lapping up the food she finds.

She has small, stubby teeth, but she doesn't use them for chewing or biting or much of anything.

Soon she ambles on, searching for more food. She goes into dense, scrubby areas, where her carapace lets her slip through tangles and prickles. Her bands allow her to bend and turn with ease.

After a while she wanders too close to a road. Suddenly there is a flash of headlights. What does the armadillo do?

She jumps!

That's what armadillos do when they are startled.
Then they run like crazy.

This armadillo is lucky. The car does not hit her.

She comes to a small river. To cross it she can hold
her breath, sink, and walk along the plants on the
bottom. Or she can gulp lots of air into her stomach,
float, and paddle along like a ball with feet.

Sometimes armadillos float on logs. People say they
may have crossed the big Mississippi River this way.
Nine-banded armadillos live in the southern United
States and all through Central and South America.

Now the armadillo looks very fat. Soon she
will have babies. To make her nest cozy for
them, she collects grass and leaves. She holds
the grass and leaves in a bundle between her
front and hind legs. Then she hops backwards.
As she hops, her tail guides her into the burrow.
She does this many times, until her nest is just
right.

In the nest, she gives birth to four baby armadillos, or pups. Each pup is exactly the same as the others. They are identical quadruplets.

Their mother's milk helps them grow. Armadillos are mammals. Mammals have hair or fur, and mammal mothers feed their young with milk from their own bodies.

The pups are lively right from birth. Their eyes are open, and they crawl all over their mother, and one another.

Their mother takes good care of them. She leaves her burrow less often now.

At first the pups' armor is soft, smooth, and shiny. It feels a little like wax. The armor will become tougher as the pups grow.

In a few months they will be big enough and strong enough to go out on their own. Until then they stay inside the burrow, drink their mother's milk, and play. They sniff one another and crawl all over each other until . . . they are all tired out. Then they snuggle up together and close their eyes.

They are ready for a good nap. Sleep tight.

THINK IT OVER

1. What is the most interesting thing you learned about an armadillo?

2. What does an armadillo look like? Tell as much as you can.

3. When does an armadillo sleep? When is it awake?

4. How does an armadillo find its food?

WRITE

Imagine that you follow the armadillo one night and take pictures. Write about what the armadillo does and when it does each thing. Draw pictures.

INSTRUCTIONS

If you should ever choose
To bathe an armadillo,
Use one bar of soap
And a whole lot of hope
And seventy-two pads of Brillo.

Shel Silverstein

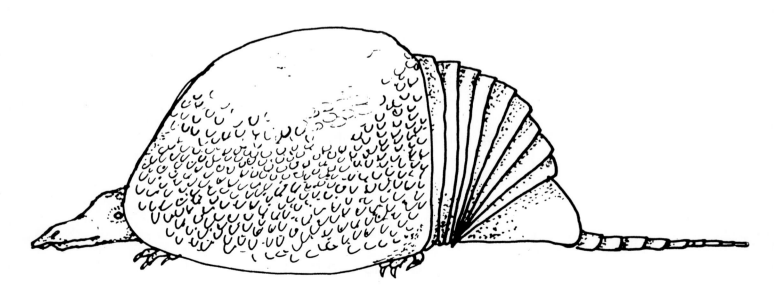

NIGHTTIME ANIMALS

How are the aardvark and the armadillo alike? How are they different?

. . . .

If you took pictures of Aardvark at night, what would he be doing?

. . . .

WRITER'S WORKSHOP Why might the armadillo be awake at night? Think of some funny reasons like those in "Awful Aardvark." Write a story about why the armadillo acts as she does. Then make your story into a book to share with your classmates.

44

SILLY SNAKES

Have you ever seen a real snake? What was it like? Most people do not think snakes are funny. But in the following story and riddles, you will find that some snakes can be very silly!

C O N T E N T S

The Day Jimmy's Boa Ate the Wash

by TRINKA HAKES NOBLE

pictures by STEVEN KELLOGG

"How was your class trip
to the farm?"

"Oh . . . boring . . . kind of
dull . . . until the cow started
crying."

"A cow . . . crying?"
"Yeah, you see, a haystack
fell on her."

"But a haystack doesn't
just fall over."

"It does if a farmer crashes into it with his tractor."

"Oh, come on, a farmer wouldn't do that."

"He would if he were too busy yelling at the pigs to get off our school bus."

"What were the pigs doing on the bus?"
"Eating our lunches."

"Why were they eating your lunches?"
"Because we threw their corn at each other,
and they didn't have anything else to eat."

50

"Well, that makes sense, but why were you throwing corn?"

"Because we ran out of eggs."

"Out of eggs? Why were you throwing eggs?"

51

"Because of the boa constrictor."

"THE BOA CONSTRICTOR!"

"Yeah, Jimmy's pet boa constrictor."

"What was Jimmy's pet boa constrictor doing on the farm?"

"Oh, he brought it to meet all the farm animals, but the chickens didn't like it."

53

"You mean he took it into the henhouse?"

"Yeah, and the chickens started squawking and flying around."

"Go on, go on. What happened?"

55

"Well, one hen got excited and laid an egg, and it landed on Jenny's head."

"The hen?"

"No, the egg. And it broke—yucky—all over her hair."

"What did she do?"

"She got mad because she thought Tommy threw it, so she threw one at him."

"What did Tommy do?"

"Oh, he ducked and the egg hit Marianne in the face.

"So she threw one at Jenny but she missed and hit Jimmy, who dropped his boa constrictor."

"Oh, and I know, the next thing you knew, everyone was throwing eggs, right?"

"Right."

"And when you ran out of eggs, you threw the pigs' corn, right?"

"Right again."

"Well, what finally stopped it?"

"Well, we heard the farmer's wife screaming."

"Why was she screaming?"

"We never found out, because Mrs. Stanley made us get on the bus, and we sort of left in a hurry without the boa constrictor."

"I bet Jimmy was sad because he left his pet boa constrictor."

"Oh, not really. We left in such a hurry that one of the pigs didn't get off the bus, so now he's got a pet pig."

"Boy, that sure sounds like an exciting trip."

"Yeah, I suppose, if you're the kind of kid who likes class trips to the farm."

THINK IT OVER

1. What starts all the trouble at the farm?

2. What things happen after Jimmy brings his boa into the henhouse?

3. Why are the pigs eating the children's lunches on the bus?

4. What do you think will happen to Jimmy's boa?

WRITE

What will happen now that Jimmy has a pet pig? Write more to add on to the story. Tell about the funny things that happen.

STEVEN KELLOGG

When I illustrate a story written by another author, like *The Day Jimmy's Boa Ate the Wash*, I pretend I'm seeing the words in my head like the pictures in a movie. I try to think up pictures that will tell different things from the words. Sometimes the author lets me have some input into the story. For instance, *The Day Jimmy's Boa Ate the Wash* was originally called *Our Class Trip to the Farm*. After I drew the boa eating the laundry on the clothesline, I thought, "Hey, that would be a good title for the book." Happily, the author, Trinka Hakes Noble, agreed.

SNAKEY RIDDLES

What kind of shoes do reptiles wear?

Snakers!

What kind of slippers do snakes wear?

Water moccasins!

SNAKEY RIDDLES
BY KATY HALL AND LISA EISENBERG
PICTURES BY SIMMS TABACK

SILLY SNAKES

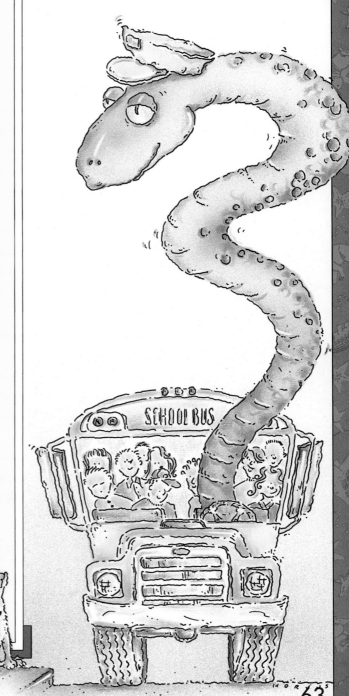

Which part of the story or which riddle do you think is the funniest? Why?

. . . .

Make up a riddle about Jimmy's boa. Tell it to a classmate.

. . . .

WRITER'S WORKSHOP What if Jimmy gets his boa back? Where else might Jimmy, his boa, and his classmates go on a trip? Write a story about another funny adventure they have. Try to write about funny things that cause other funny things to happen. Draw pictures to go with your story. You may want to make your story into a book to share with your classmates.

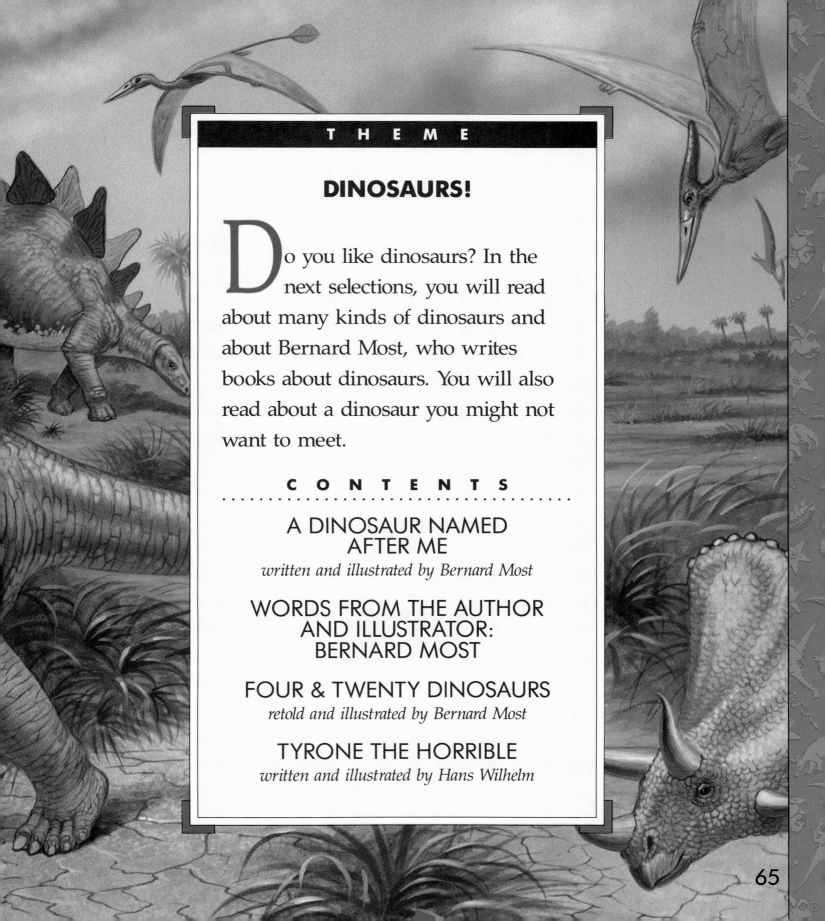

DINOSAURS!

Do you like dinosaurs? In the next selections, you will read about many kinds of dinosaurs and about Bernard Most, who writes books about dinosaurs. You will also read about a dinosaur you might not want to meet.

CONTENTS

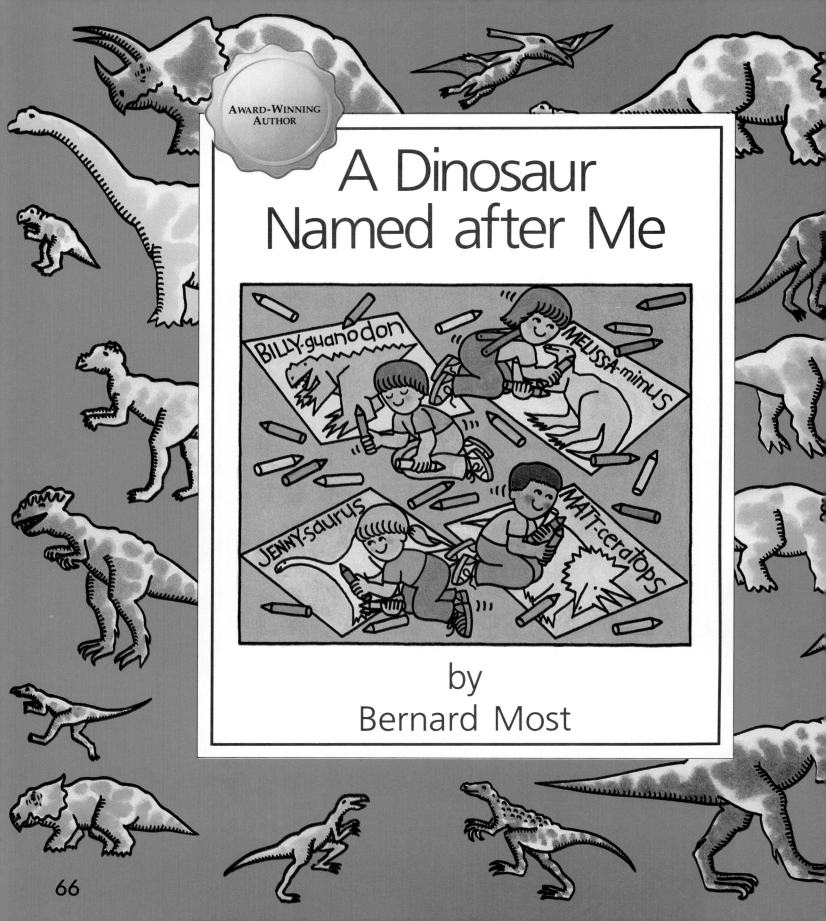

A Dinosaur Named after Me

by
Bernard Most

Pentaceratops (PEN-ta-ser-a-tops)

My favorite dinosaur was Triceratops . . . until I read about Pentaceratops. Its name means "five-horned face" because it had two more horns than Triceratops. It also had a much larger frill. Since I was born on the fifth day of the fifth month, five is my lucky number. This dinosaur should be named BEN-taceratops!

Ben

Apatosaurus (ah-PAT-a-saw-russ)

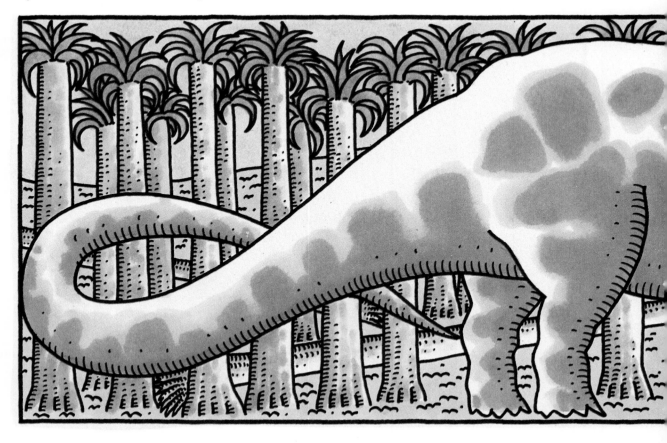

My favorite dinosaur is Apatosaurus.
This is the correct scientific name for
Brontosaurus, which was thought to be
a new dinosaur when it was discovered.
But scientists now think it is the same
as a dinosaur discovered years earlier,
Apatosaurus. I like the name A-PAT-osaurus
much better anyway.

Pat

Brontosaurus (BRON-ta-saw-russ)

Ron

My favorite dinosaur is Brontosaurus. Everyone knows this dinosaur as Brontosaurus—so why change it? Many scientists today think dinosaurs were more like mammals and birds than reptiles. But no one wants to change the name *dinosaur,* which means "terrible lizard." If you must change the name of Brontosaurus, call it RON-tosaurus!

Brachiosaurus (BRAK-ee-a-saw-russ)

My favorite dinosaur is Brachiosaurus. It was a member of the tallest dinosaur family and could reach higher than any other dinosaur. I am the tallest person in my class, and I can reach higher than anybody. I would have named Brachiosaurus after me: ZACH-iosaurus.

Zach

70

Ankylosaurus (an-KILE-a-saw-russ)

My favorite dinosaur is Ankylosaurus. Rows of bony plates and a clublike tail protected this peaceful plant eater from meat eaters. Every time I visit the museum and see a knight's armor, I think about this largest armored dinosaur. But a much better name would be HANK-ylosaurus!

Hank

71

Microvenator (mike-row-ven-AY-tor)

My favorite dinosaur is Microvenator, or "small hunter." This turkey-sized meat eater was good at catching its dinner because it was very fast and had grasping claws. I'm a small hunter, too. I'm good at catching my friends when we play hide-and-seek. "Ready or not, here comes MIKE-rovenator!"

Mike

Maiasaura (my-a-SAW-ra)

My favorite dinosaur is Maiasaura. Named "good mother lizard" because it was found near a nest with fifteen baby dinosaurs, scientists think it brought food to its babies and took good care of them. Mom says I take good care of my baby brother. She says this dinosaur's name should be MARY-asaura.

Mary

Stegosaurus (STEG-a-saw-russ)

My favorite dinosaur is Stegosaurus. Scientists think the large plates that covered its back were for protection and made Stegosaurus look larger to meat-eating dinosaurs—just like my shoulder pads protect me and make me look larger to opposing teams. My friends renamed Stegosaurus GREG-osaurus.

Greg

74

Dravidosaurus (dra-VID-a-saw-russ)

My favorite dinosaur is Dravidosaurus. It was a member of the Stegosaurus family but one of the littlest, only ten feet long. It's like a little brother to Stegosaurus. I'm Greg's little brother, so if they change Stegosaurus to GREG-osaurus, I hope they change Dravidosaurus to DAVID-osaurus!

David

75

Dinosaurs
(DIE-na-sawrs)

Diane

I don't have a favorite dinosaur, because they are all my favorites. I love reading about every one of them. If I had my way, I would change their name from dinosaurs to DIANE-osaurs.

Think about your favorite dinosaur. Wouldn't you like a dinosaur named after YOU?

76

THINK IT OVER

1. How were all the dinosaurs alike?

2. Which dinosaur is your favorite? Why?

3. How did some dinosaurs protect themselves from enemies?

WRITE

You just saw a dinosaur! What kind was it? Write a story about it to read on a class news show.

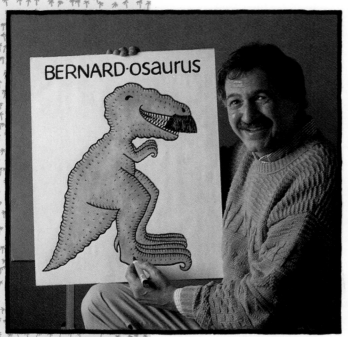

BERNARD·osaurus

Photo by Donato Leo

Words from the Author and Illustrator:

BERNARD MOST

I became interested in dinosaurs when my son Glen was in second grade. His teacher asked him to write down three wishes. One of his wishes was that the dinosaurs would come back to life. At the time, I was trying to come up with an idea for a picture book. When I heard Glen's wish, it was as if a light bulb went on over my head. I didn't know very much about dinosaurs, so I had to do a lot of research. I had to learn to draw dinosaurs so they looked like dinosaurs. My first tries weren't very good.

I got the idea for *A Dinosaur Named After Me* from autographing books. Sometimes people would say, "Make this out to Matthew-saurus." I decided to take some real dinosaur names and put them together with children's names.

When I'm not writing, I spend time with my tropical fish collection. I have a houseful of fish tanks. My other son, Eric, got me interested in fish. My other hobbies are music and making home videos.

The best thing about writing is seeing all the ideas and pages and pictures come together in an actual book. My favorite dinosaur is triceratops. I like to visit schools and draw a picture of a triceratops, and then underneath, I write READING IS TOPS!

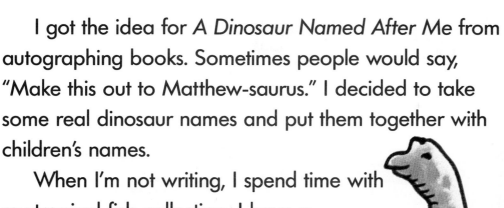

Four & Twenty

Sing a song of sixpence,
A pocketful of rye;
Four and twenty dinosaurs,
Baked in a pie.

Dinosaurs

by Bernard Most

When the pie was opened,
They all began to sing;
Was that not a dainty dish,
To set before the king?

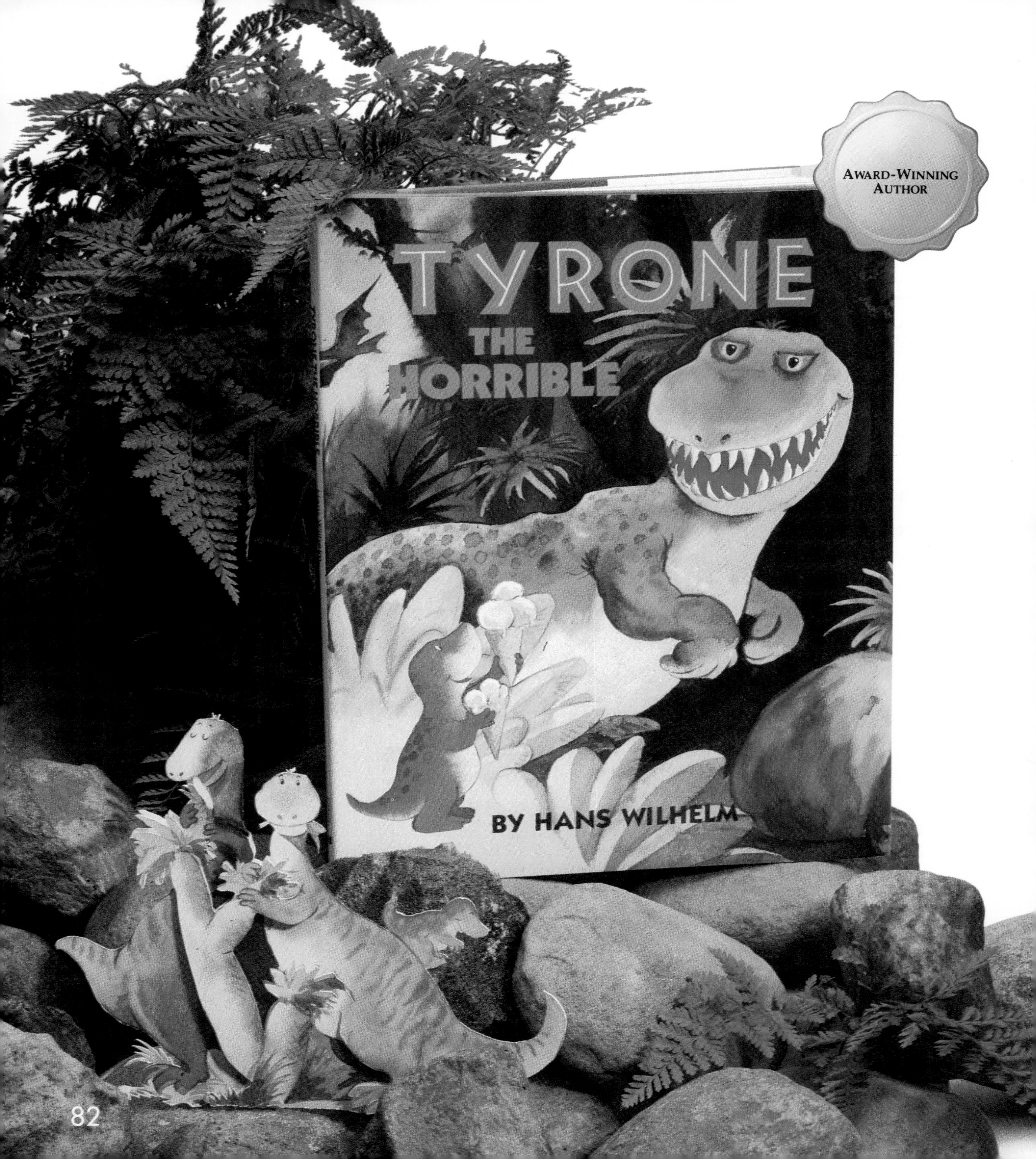
AWARD-WINNING AUTHOR
TYRONE
THE
HORRIBLE
BY HANS WILHELM

Boland was a little dinosaur. He lived with his mother and father in a great swamp forest.

There were a lot of dinosaur children in Boland's neighborhood.

They played together every day, and Boland was friendly with all of them—all of them, except one. . . .

His name was Tyrone—or Tyrone the Horrible, as he was usually called.

He was just a kid himself, but he was much bigger and stronger than most of the others.

He was a real bully if you ever saw one. In fact, he was the world's first big bully!

Tyrone especially liked to pick on Boland. He punched and teased him and always stole his snack or sandwich.

Boland tried to stay out of Tyrone's way, but it seemed that no matter where he went, Tyrone was waiting for him.

Night after night, Boland had a hard time getting to sleep. He kept thinking of ways to avoid Tyrone. It seemed hopeless.

Boland's playmates tried to help.

"You have to get Tyrone to be your friend," Terry said to Boland one day.

"That's easier said than done," said Boland. "How do you make friends with someone who has been hurting and teasing you all your life?"

"You have to give him a present and show him you care," Terry said.

Boland thought for a while. What kind of present could he give Tyrone? Then he remembered how Tyrone was always taking his snacks and sandwiches. "A present for Tyrone?" he said. "Well, at least it's worth a try."

That afternoon, Boland went looking for Tyrone. "Here," he said in his friendliest voice. "It's such a hot day, I thought you might like a nice ice-cream cone."

Tyrone looked at Boland for a moment. Then he smiled a nasty smile. "Ice cream for me? How sweet!"

Tyrone grabbed the cone. Then he turned it upside down and squashed it on Boland's head.

"Ha ha ha!" Tyrone laughed and walked away.

Boland could hear Tyrone's laughter for a long time, echoing through the forest.

The next day, Boland told his friend Stella what had happened.

"You are taking this too seriously," Stella said. "Don't pay any attention to that big bully when he tries to tease you. Just stay cool. That's the only thing he'll understand."

"Staying cool when you are scared is not easy," Boland said. "But I will try."

And so the next time Boland met Tyrone, he stayed cool.

"Hi, Lizardhead!" roared Tyrone as Boland walked by. "How about MY sandwich?"

Boland did not pay any attention and didn't even try to run away. He kept on walking.

"I guess I'll have to help myself again," Tyrone said. He stomped on Boland's tail until Boland let go of the sandwich.

Boland tried not to show his tears. But it hurt a lot.

When Boland's friends found out what Tyrone had done, they were furious.

"It's time to fight back!" Stego said. "Tyrone has given you enough trouble. You must stand up to him and show him you are a dinosaur, too. You can win any fight against him. Tyrone just has a big mouth, that's all."

Boland was angry, too. "You're right!" he said. "Maybe I should fight him and stop this nonsense once and for all."

"Well," Stego said, "let's do it right now!"

The four friends marched off to find Tyrone.

Boland stood up and faced Tyrone the Horrible. "Listen, you brute," he said. "I have had enough of your bullying. Come on and fight!"

Tyrone took one look at Boland, then grinned and said, "Okay, if that's what you want."

It was a very short fight.

Little Boland had no chance against his big enemy.

"I'm sorry," Stego said. "That was not a very good idea. You'd better give up. Some bullies you just can't beat. You have to learn to live with them, whether you like it or not."

But Boland did not like it. "There just has to be a way to beat a bully," he thought.

He was still thinking as the moon came out and the stars filled the sky. Suddenly he smiled a big smile. "That's it!" he said to himself. Then he curled up and was soon fast asleep.

The next morning Boland took his sandwich and went off into the swamp forest as usual. It wasn't long before he ran into Tyrone.

"Another snack for me?" roared Tyrone. "I hope it's something good!" And with that he swiped the sandwich out of Boland's hand and swallowed it with one big gulp.

Boland walked on as fast as he could.

Suddenly he heard a terrible scream.

"AAaaaaaarghhhhhh!" It was Tyrone. Huge flames were coming out of his mouth. "HELP, I'm burning," he cried. "I'm dying! I'm poisoned! HELP, HEEEEEELP!"

"Nonsense!" Boland said with a laugh. "It was only a sandwich. I didn't know you were so sensitive. I happen to like *double-thick-red-hot-pepper-sandwiches.* Too bad you don't." He turned around and went off, leaving the moaning and groaning Tyrone behind.

From then on, Tyrone stayed as far away from Boland as he could.

Boland played happily with his friends in the swamp forest all day, and he never had trouble falling asleep at night.

When much, much later some scientists found Tyrone the Horrible, he looked a little different—but he still had that nasty smile on his face.

THINK IT OVER

1. What is Boland's problem? How does he finally solve the problem?

2. Do you think Boland's friends give him good advice about how to solve the problem? Explain your answer.

3. What would you do about Tyrone if you were Boland?

4. Why do you think Tyrone acts as he does?

WRITE

Imagine that you are Boland or one of Boland's friends. Write a letter to Tyrone. Tell him how you and he can become good friends.

DINOSAURS!

What kind of dinosaur do you think Tyrone is? What kind do you think Boland is?

. . . .

What do you think Bernard Most would write about Tyrone?

. . . .

WRITER'S WORKSHOP If you could name a dinosaur after you, which one would it be? Draw a picture of your dinosaur. Then write about it. Describe your dinosaur by telling what it looks like and how it acts. Be sure to include lots of details. Put your work into a class dinosaur book.

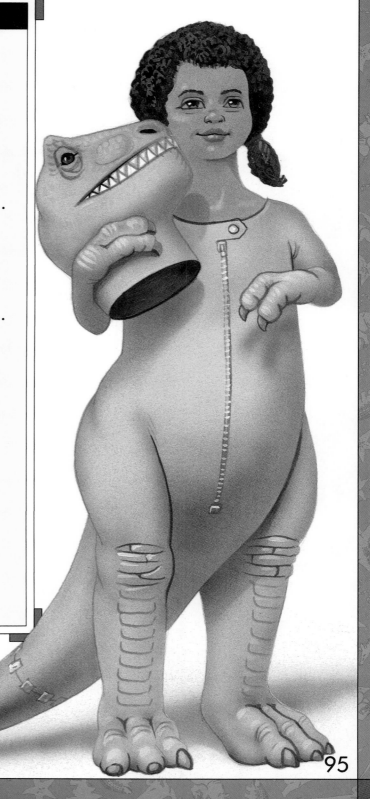

95

CONNECTIONS

WHERE THE WILD THINGS HIDE AT NIGHT

Maurice Sendak's father was a great storyteller. At night, he told his son Jewish tales that he had heard long ago in Poland.

These stories made Maurice decide to write books himself. He spent his free time writing and drawing pictures. When he grew up, he drew pictures for other writers' books. He wrote his own books, too. One of his best early books was <u>Where the Wild Things Are</u>. It won many prizes. Look at the picture that shows some wild things. Do you find them scary or funny—or both?

■ Draw your own picture of some unusual wild animals. Make up a story about them.

NIGHT ANIMALS

What do animals do when they stay awake at night? Where do they go? With a partner, pick an animal that you might see out at night. Find out facts about it. Then tell your classmates what you learned.

A drawing like this one might help you record the facts you find.

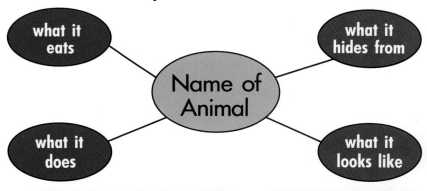

I WENT TO THE ANIMAL FAIR

With a group of your classmates, put together a book of songs about unusual or funny animals. Draw a picture to go with each song. With your group, sing one of the songs for your classmates.

It was like being in our own little world.
Carmen Lomas Garza

What is it like in your own little world? Where do you live? What do you eat? Maybe there is a special meal you and your family enjoy. In Japan, families have special foods for every season. You might enjoy the *shabu-shabu* they eat in winter. Read more about it and about cultures around the world in this unit.

BOOKSHELF

THE TERRIBLE EEK

RETOLD BY PATRICIA COMPTON

In this Japanese tale, a lucky mistake keeps a boy and his father safe from a thief and a wolf.

HBJ LIBRARY BOOK

I HATE ENGLISH!

BY ELLEN LEVINE

When Mei Mei moves from Hong Kong to New York, she will not speak English. She is afraid she will lose the Chinese part of herself. At last a special teacher gives Mei Mei the gift of English. ALA NOTABLE BOOK

A DROP OF HONEY
BY DJEMMA BIDER

A girl falls asleep and dreams about the trouble that just one drop of honey can cause. Her dream teaches her that a little problem can turn into big trouble.

ABUELA
BY ARTHUR DORROS

A girl imagines an adventure with her *abuela*, "grandmother" in Spanish. The two have the time of their lives flying over the city of New York. AWARD-WINNING AUTHOR

ANTARCTICA
BY HELEN COWCHER

Penguins, seals, and other animals live in Antarctica. One day humans arrive on the icy shores. Have these visitors come in peace?

101

FAMILY FUN

Are there special things that you like to do with your family? Do you like to hear grown-ups tell about when they were little? In the next stories, you will read about the fun two people had when they were children.

C O N T E N T S

written by Charlotte Pomerantz
illustrated by Frané Lessac

The Chalk Doll

Rose had a cold.
The doctor said to stay in bed
and try to nap during the day.
Rose's mother kissed her
and drew the curtains.
"You forgot to kiss me," said Rose.
"I did kiss you," said Mother.
"You didn't kiss me good night."
Mother went over and kissed her.
"Good night, Rosy," she said.
"I need my bear," said Rose.
"Your bear?" said Mother.
"You haven't slept with your bear
since you were little."
"I'm still little," said Rose.
She hugged her bear.
"Mommy," she said, "did you have
a bear when you were
a little girl in Jamaica?"
"No," said Mother. "But I had
a rag doll."

The Rag Doll

"I took a piece of material and folded
it over once.
With a pencil, I drew the outline
of the doll on the material.
Then I cut along the outline and sewed
the two sides together.
Before I finished sewing up the head,
I stuffed the doll with bits of rags."
"Did you like your rag doll, Mommy?"
"Yes, Rose, because I made it.
But I liked the dolls in
the shop windows more.
We called them chalk dolls."
"Did you ever have a chalk doll, Mommy?"

The Chalk Doll

"Yes, my aunt worked for a family
who gave her a chalk doll,
and my aunt gave it to me.
The doll was missing an arm,
and her nose was broken."
"Poor doll," said Rose.
"Oh, no," said Mother.
"To me she was the most perfect
doll in the world."
"That's because she belonged to you,"
said Rose.
Mother smiled.
"Now try and rest," she said.
"Tell me another story," said Rose.
"I can't think of any," said Mother.
"Tell me the story of your birthday party."
Mother looked puzzled.
"My birthday party?
We didn't have birthday parties."
"What about the three pennies?" said Rose.
"Oh," said Mother. "That time."

The Birthday Party

"On the day I was seven years old,
my mother gave me three pennies.
I had never had so much money.
The pennies were cool and smooth in my hand.
I went to a store and bought
a little round piece of sponge cake
for a penny. Then I went to
another store and bought a
penny's worth of powdered sugar.
In the third store, I bought six
tiny candies for a penny.
When I got home, I sprinkled
powdered sugar on the top."
"I bet I know what happened then,"
said Rose. "Five friends came over.
You cut the cake into six little pieces
and you had a party. . . . But Mommy,
you didn't get any presents."
"No, I never did."
"Never, never?"
"Well," said Mother, "I did,
if you count the pink taffeta dress."

The Pink Taffeta Dress

"My mother was a seamstress. She worked
at home, sewing for other people.
One year she brought home some pink taffeta.
Pink taffeta was my favorite.
She said she would try and make
me a dress for my birthday.
But she was so busy sewing dresses for
other people that weeks and weeks went by
and she still hadn't touched the pink taffeta.
The night before my birthday,
I went to bed hoping she would
make the dress while I was asleep.
But when I woke up,
the pink taffeta material was still there.
I went to the yard and cried."
Rose leaned over and hugged her mother.
"Poor Mommy," she said.
"Did she ever make the dress?"
"Yes," said Mother. "She finished the dress
a month after my birthday.
It was the most beautiful dress I ever had."
"What kind of shoes did you
wear with it, Mommy?"
"No shoes, Rose.

We only wore shoes
to church on Sunday."
"You mean you went to school barefoot?"
"Yes," said Mother. "Nobody
wore shoes except the teacher. . . .
But I *did* wear high heels."

High Heels

"The road to and from school was paved with tar,
and there were mango trees on both sides.
We ate the sweet fruit and dropped the pits.
They dried in the sun. We took the dried pits
and rubbed them into the tar on the road.
The tar was soft and sticky.
After we rubbed the mango pits
in the tar, we pressed the sticky pits
against the heels of our feet until they stuck.
Then we walked home clickety click
clacking on our mango heels." Rose smiled.
"Clickety click clack," she said.
"You had fun when you were
a little girl, didn't you, Mommy?"
"Yes, Rosy. I did."
"Do I have as much fun as you did?" Rose asked.
"Mm," said Mother,
"what do you think?"
"I think I have fun too," said Rose.
"But there is one thing I'd like to have
that you had." Rose got out of bed and
went to the sewing basket in the hallway.
She took out a needle and thread, a pair
of scissors, and some scraps of material.
"What are you doing?" said Mother.

"I'm getting everything ready."

"Ready for what, Rose?"

"Ready to make a rag doll."

"But Rose," said Mother,

"you have so many dolls."

"I know," said Rose.

"But they are all chalk dolls.
I've never had a rag doll."
Mother laughed.
"Poor Rosy," she said.
And together they made a rag doll.

THINK IT OVER

1. What things did Rose's mother do as a child?

2. What do you think would be most fun about growing up in Jamaica as Rose's mother did?

3. Why did Rose's mother think that the broken chalk doll was perfect?

4. How do you know that Rose has heard the story about the birthday party before?

WRITE

Write about your own favorite birthday.

SO WILL I
by Charlotte Zolotow

My grandfather remembers long ago
the white Queen Anne's lace that grew wild.
He remembers the buttercups and goldenrod
from when he was a child.

He remembers long ago
the white snow falling falling.
He remembers the bluebird and thrush
at twilight
calling, calling.

He remembers long ago
the new moon in the summer sky.
He remembers the wind in the trees
and its long, rising sigh.
And so will I
        so will I.

Catching Minnows-Town Meadows, Kent
by John Pedder (1850–1929)
Waterhouse and Dodd Gallery, London

The pictures in this book are all painted from my memories of growing up in Kingsville, Texas, near the border with Mexico. From the time I was a young girl I always dreamed of becoming an artist. I practiced drawing every day; I studied art in school; and I finally did become an artist. My family has inspired and encouraged me for all these years. This is my book of family pictures.

Oranges

We were always going to my grandparents' house, so whatever they were involved in we would get involved in. In this picture my grandmother is hanging up the laundry. We told her that the oranges needed picking so she said, "Well, go ahead and pick some." Before she knew it, she had too many oranges to hold in her hands, so she made a basket out of her apron. That's my brother up in the tree, picking oranges. The rest of us are picking up the ones that he dropped on the ground.

Cakewalk

Cakewalk was a game to raise money to send Mexican Americans to the university. You paid 25 cents to stand on a number. When the music started, you walked around and around. When the music stopped, whatever number you happened to step on was your number. Then one of the ladies in the center would pick out a number from the can. If you were standing on the winning number, you would win a cake. That's my mother in the center of the circle in the pink and black dress. My father is serving punch. I'm the little girl in front of the store scribbling on the sidewalk with a twig.

Making Tamales

This is a scene from my parents' kitchen. Everybody is making tamales. My grandfather is wearing blue overalls and a blue shirt. I'm right next to him with my sister Margie. We're helping to soak the dried leaves from the corn. My mother is spreading the cornmeal dough on the leaves and my aunt and uncle are spreading meat on the dough. My grandmother is lining up the rolled and folded tamales ready for cooking. In some families just the women make tamales, but in our family everybody helps.

Birthday Party

That's me hitting the piñata at my sixth birthday party. It was also my brother's fourth birthday. My mother made a big birthday party for us and invited all kinds of friends, cousins and neighborhood kids.

You can't see the piñata when you're trying to hit it, because your eyes are covered with a handkerchief. My father is pulling the rope that makes the piñata go up and down. He will make sure that everybody has a chance to hit it at least once. Somebody will end up breaking it, and that's when all the candies will fall out and all the kids will run and try to grab them.

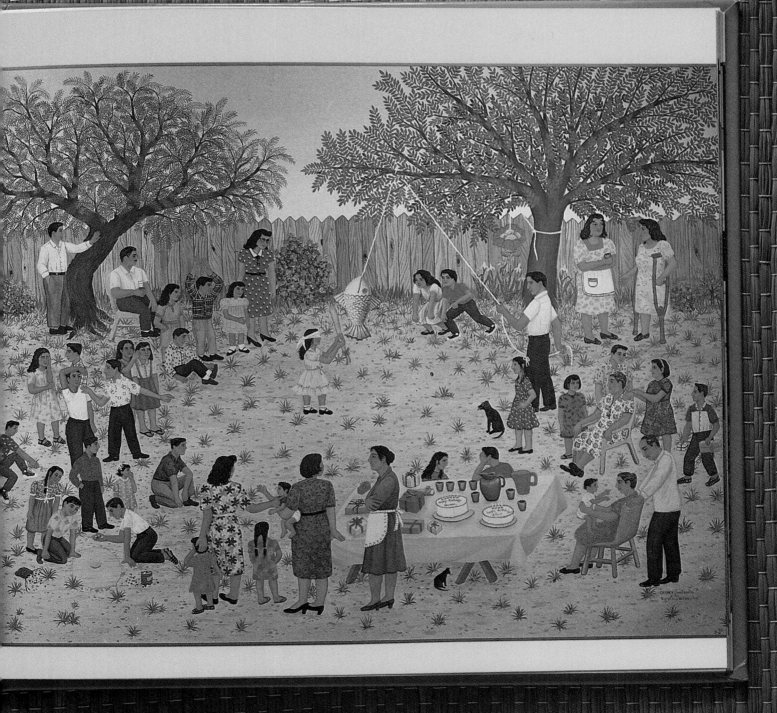

Watermelon

It's a hot summer evening. The whole family's on the front porch. My grandfather had brought us some watermelons that afternoon. My father cut the watermelon and gave each one of us a slice. It was fun to sit out there. The light was so bright on the porch that you couldn't see beyond the edge of the lit area. It was like being in our own little world.

THINK IT OVER

1. Why did Carmen Lomas Garza choose to draw and tell about her family?

2. What was the reason for having the cakewalk?

WRITE

Carmen dreamed about becoming an artist. Write a paragraph that tells what you dream about becoming someday.

WORDS ABOUT THE AUTHOR AND ILLUSTRATOR:

CARMEN LOMAS GARZA

Each person in her paintings is a family member or neighbor in real life.

Carmen Lomas Garza grew up in Texas. When she was thirteen, she knew she wanted to be an artist. Carmen practiced drawing on the back of her homework papers. She drew anyone who would let her. If there was no one to draw, Carmen drew plants, objects, even her own hands.

Today, Carmen Lomas Garza is one of the finest Mexican American painters. She painted all the scenes in "Family Pictures" from memory. Each person in her paintings is a family member or neighbor in real life.

When Carmen isn't painting, she loves to visit her artist friends, go to their art shows, or go dancing with her husband.

FAMILY FUN

Do you think that Rose's mother would enjoy Carmen Lomas Garza's birthday party? Explain your answer.

....

Rose's mother says that she had fun when she was a child. Do you think that the author of "Family Pictures" had fun as a child? Tell why you think as you do.

....

WRITER'S WORKSHOP When you grow up, what special memory from your childhood will you share with others? Write some sentences describing something that has happened to you. Use colorful words to make your writing as interesting as possible. Share your writing with a classmate.

131

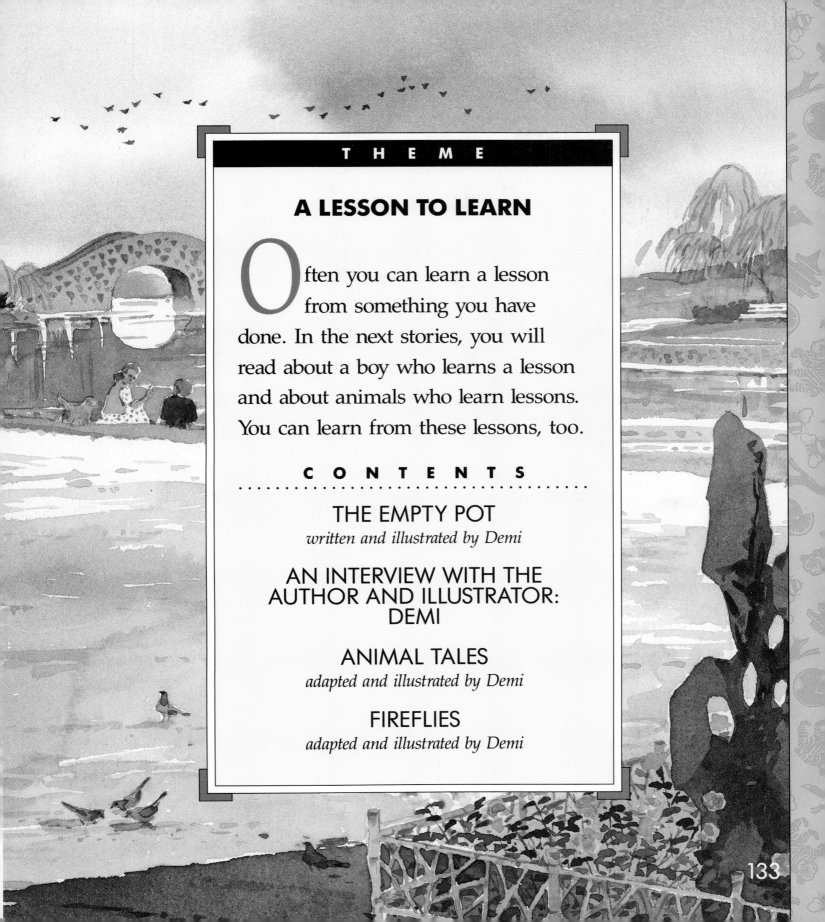

A LESSON TO LEARN

Often you can learn a lesson from something you have done. In the next stories, you will read about a boy who learns a lesson and about animals who learn lessons. You can learn from these lessons, too.

C O N T E N T S

THE EMPTY POT

TEACHERS'
CHOICE

CHILDREN'S CHOICE

NOTABLE TRADE
BOOK IN SOCIAL
STUDIES

DEMI

A long time ago in China there was a boy named Ping who loved flowers. Anything he planted burst into bloom. Up came flowers, bushes, and even big fruit trees, as if by magic!

Everyone in the kingdom loved flowers too. They planted them everywhere, and the air smelled like perfume.

The Emperor loved birds and animals, but flowers most of all, and he tended his own garden every day.

But the Emperor was very old. He needed to choose a successor to the throne. Who would his successor be? And how would the Emperor choose? Because the Emperor loved flowers so much, he decided to let the flowers choose.

The next day a proclamation was issued: All the children in the land were to come to the palace. There they would be given special flower seeds by the Emperor. "Whoever can show me their best in a year's time," he said, "will succeed me to the throne."

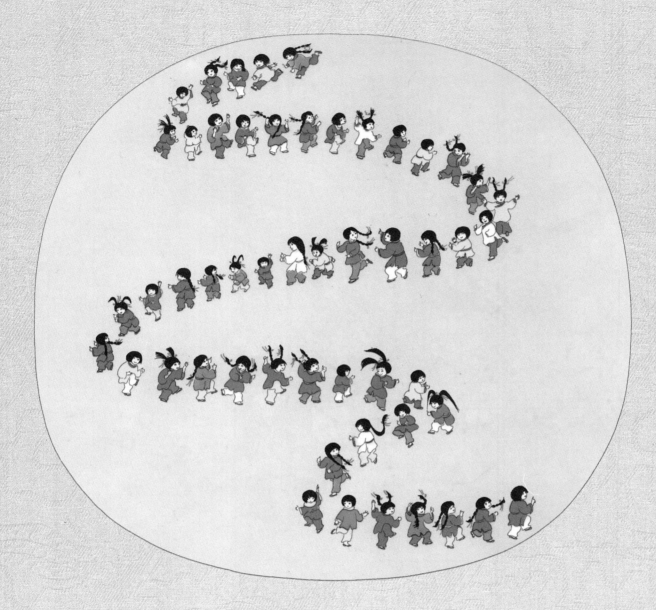

This news created great excitement throughout the land! Children from all over the country swarmed to the palace to get their flower seeds.

All the parents wanted their children to be chosen Emperor, and all the children hoped they would be chosen too!

When Ping received his seed from the Emperor, he was the happiest child of all. He was sure he could grow the most beautiful flower.

Ping filled a flowerpot with rich soil. He planted the seed in it very carefully. He watered it every day.

He couldn't wait to see it sprout, grow, and blossom into a beautiful flower!

Day after day passed, but nothing grew in his pot.

Ping was very worried. He put new soil into a bigger pot. Then he transferred the seed into the rich black soil.

Another two months he waited. Still nothing happened. By and by the whole year passed.

Spring came, and all the children put on their best clothes to greet the Emperor. They rushed to the palace with their beautiful flowers, eagerly hoping to be chosen.

Ping was ashamed of his empty pot. He thought the other children would laugh at him because for once he couldn't get a flower to grow.

142

His clever friend ran by, holding a great big plant.
"Ping!" he said. "You're not really going to the
Emperor with an empty pot, are you? Couldn't you
grow a great big flower like mine?"

"I've grown lots of flowers better than yours," Ping
said. "It's just this seed that won't grow."

Ping's father overheard this and said, "You did your best, and your best is good enough to present to the Emperor."

Holding the empty pot in his hands, Ping went straight away to the palace.

The Emperor was looking at the flowers slowly, one by one. How beautiful all the flowers were! But the Emperor was frowning and did not say a word. Finally he came to Ping.

Ping hung his head in shame, expecting to be punished. The Emperor asked him, "Why did you bring an empty pot?"

Ping started to cry and replied, "I planted the seed you gave me and I watered it every day, but it didn't sprout. I put it in a better pot with better soil, but still it didn't sprout! I tended it all year long, but nothing grew. So today I had to bring an empty pot without a flower. It was the best I could do."

When the Emperor heard these words, a smile
slowly spread over his face, and he put his arm around
Ping. Then he exclaimed to one and all, "I have found
him! I have found the one person worthy of being
Emperor!

"Where you got your seeds from, I do not know.
For the seeds I gave you had all been cooked. So it
was impossible for any of them to grow.

"I admire Ping's great courage to appear before me with the empty truth, and now I reward him with my entire kingdom and make him Emperor of all the land!"

THINK IT OVER

1. What lesson can be learned from this story?

2. Why does the Emperor give seeds to the children?

3. How does Ping try to get his seed to grow?

WRITE

Write an ad the Emperor would place in the local newspaper to find his successor.

**Ms. Cooper, a
writer, asked
Demi some
questions about
her stories.**

demi

Cooper: Many of your stories take place in Asia. Is that a special place for you?

Demi: Oh yes. My husband, Tze-Si Huang, is from China, so that country is very special to me.

Cooper: Did you first become interested in China when you met your husband?

Demi: No. Many years before, even as a child, I was drawn to things of Asia. We had a Chinese rug in our house, a Ming vase with butterflies, and a carved Chinese chess set. All those things attracted me as a child.

148

Cooper: Where did you get the story of
The Empty Pot?

Demi: From my husband. One night, while he
was cooking supper, he told me this
tale. I rushed to get a pencil to write
it down. The doorbell kept ringing,
and he had to keep starting over, but
eventually, I got it on paper.

Cooper: Was this a story he
had heard as a boy?

Demi: Yes. This isn't the first tale he's told me.
I've used several of them in my books. They are
stories that were passed down to him
by his grandmother.

Animal Tales

ADAPTED AND
ILLUSTRATED BY

demi

FROM A CHINESE ZOO

FABLES AND
PROVERBS

One day a big brown bear woke up and smelled some honey. Immediately he went outside and sniffed his way to a giant honeycomb, which was guarded by many bees. He bit off a huge chunk of the comb and ran off with it in his mouth. The bees buzzed right after him, and each one stung him on the nose. "You stupid bear," they said. "Why did you take the honey when all of us were right there watching you do it?" "When I took the honey, I did not notice any of you," said the big brown bear. "I saw only the honey."

We frequently see only what we want to see.

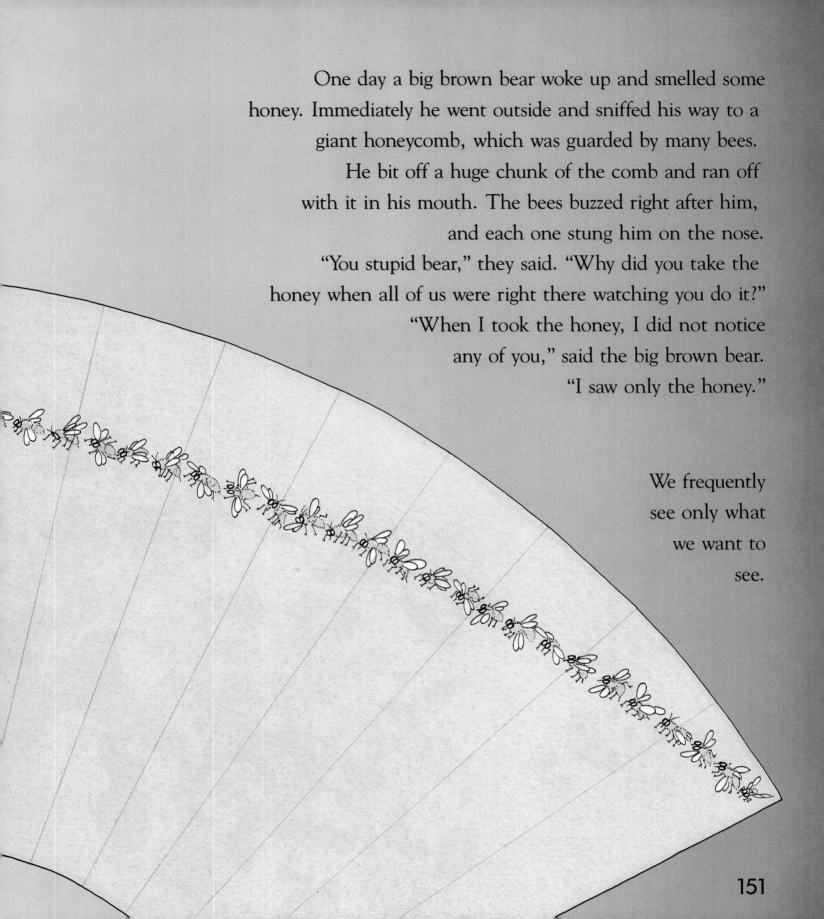

151

When the tiger was out hunting one day deep in
the forest, he caught a fox.

As he prepared to eat his prey, the fox said to the
tiger, "You must not eat me. I am the king
of the forest. Come with me and I
will show you how the other
animals fear me."

When the other animals saw the big tiger following the fox, they scattered in many different directions.

"I see what you mean," said the tiger, not realizing it was from him, not the fox, that the animals were fleeing. "I'd better find something else to eat."

Small creatures must live by their wits.

Fireflies

from <u>DRAGON KITES AND DRAGONFLIES</u>
adapted and illustrated by Demi

Fireflies, fireflies,
Tiny lanterns in the sky,
You fly up high,
You fly down low;
Now on sister's
Dress you glow.

154

A LESSON TO LEARN

How is Ping like the animals in "Animal Tales"?

....

Why do you think the Emperor cooks the seeds so none of them will grow? Why doesn't he give the children good seeds and make the child who grows the best flower his successor?

....

WRITER'S WORKSHOP What kind of ruler do you think you would be? How would you choose your successor? Write a story about yourself, Emperor ___?___ or Empress ___?___ (fill in your name). Read your story aloud to your classmates.

HELPING HANDS

Can you think of a time when you made someone smile? Maybe you shared something special or gave help when it was needed. In the stories you will read next, the people who lend a helping hand make everyone else very happy.

C O N T E N T S

157

STONE SOUP

A Russian folktale by James Buechler
illustrated by Keith Baker

CHARACTERS

Sergeant

Petya

Sasha

Olga, a seamstress

Dmitri, a carpenter

Anna, a baker

Marya

Villagers

Time: *Two hundred years ago.*

Setting: *A village street in old Russia. Nearby is a stream with stones in it. Dmitri, Olga, and Anna are hard at work in their houses. Three soldiers are walking down the street by the houses. One soldier carries a knapsack, and one carries a large kettle.*

Sergeant: Cheer up, Petya and Sasha! We've come
through the forest safely. I'm sure the people of this village
will share their dinner with us.

Sasha: I hope so. My stomach is empty. It feels like a cave.

Sergeant: I'll knock on this door.

Olga: Who is it?

Sergeant: It's only three loyal soldiers, tramping home
across Russia. Can you spare us some food, good woman?

Olga: Food! No, I have nothing. Our harvest was bad.

Petya: I'll try knocking at this door. Hello in there!

Anna: What is it you want?

Petya: We'd like some supper, if you have any. We are three loyal soldiers tramping home across Russia.

Anna: I am sorry to see you so hungry, but you have come to the wrong place. It is everyone for himself in these times!

Sasha: Let us try this house. Maybe our luck will be better here.

Dmitri: Who is it? Sensible men are inside their houses, working.

Sasha: We are three soldiers, sir. It would be kind of you to share your dinner with us.

Dmitri: I have just enough dinner for myself. Go away! *(Dmitri shuts his door with a loud bang.)*

Petya: What selfish people these are!

Sasha: They do not know how to share.

Sergeant: Let's teach these peasants a lesson! We'll teach them to make stone soup.

Sasha: Aha, stone soup!

Petya: That's just the thing.

(The sergeant, Sasha, and Petya huddle together to whisper about their plan. Dmitri comes out of his shop.)

Dmitri: Are you still here, you vagabonds? If you have no food, it's your problem. Why aren't you on your way?

Sergeant: Get some firewood, Sasha! Prepare the kettle, Petya. We will build our fire here, on this spot.

(Sasha gets some firewood. Petya gets two Y-shaped sticks on which to hang the kettle.)

Petya: We can use these sticks to hang the kettle, Sergeant.

Sergeant: Perfect, Petya. Now for the stones. Go and find some tasty stones in that stream over there.

Petya: I'm on my way, Sergeant.

(Petya runs to the nearby stream and selects some stones carefully. Dmitri, Olga, Anna, Marya and the other villagers come to see what the soldiers are doing.)

Dmitri: I do not understand. What did you say you are cooking here?

Sergeant: Oh, it's just some stone soup. Tell me, what kind of stone do you like yourself? You might help us choose.

Dmitri: I! Why, I never heard of making soup from stones!

Sasha: You've never heard of stone soup? I don't believe it.

(Petya returns from the stream with a bowl of stones.)

Sergeant: Come, sir. You must dine with us. Have you some good stones there, Petya? Let Sasha choose tonight.

(Sasha looks at each stone carefully and selects a chunky one.)

Sasha: Hm-m! This chunky one will be good! Ugh! Throw that flat stone away. A flat stone has a flat taste. Fill the kettle with water, Petya. My fire is ready.

(Petya fills the kettle with water. He then hangs it over the fire.)

Sergeant: Have you a spoon? We soldiers often make do with a stick. But for a guest, the soup will need proper stirring.

Dmitri: I have just the thing. It has a nice long handle. It is in perfect condition. I have not had guests in five years.

Sergeant: Splendid, you generous man!

(Dmitri goes to get the spoon from his house.)

Anna: What's this? The soldiers are making a soup from stones?

Marya: Yes! They are using stones from our own brook. That soldier put them in. I saw him myself.

Sasha: This soup smells so good. It's making me hungry!

Dmitri: Here's the spoon. Please be careful.

Sergeant: Sir, you shall be served first.

(The sergeant stirs the soup.)

Marya: I am more hungry than usual. It must be the smell of this soup they are cooking.

Anna: I must have a cold, for I can smell nothing.

Marya: Yes, I am very hungry, indeed. I have worked in the fields since morning.

Sergeant: Let's taste the soup now, Sasha and Petya.

(The soldiers each taste the soup.)

Villagers: Is it good?

Petya: It tastes very good.

Sasha: Oh, it tastes wonderful!

Sergeant: It might stand an onion, though. Onion is very good for pulling the flavor from a stone.

Olga: You know, I might find an onion in my house.

(Olga goes to get some onions.)

Sasha: It could stand a bit of carrot as well.

Anna: Perhaps I could fetch some carrots for this soup.

Sergeant: That is gracious of you. Will you bring a bowl for yourself, as well? You must dine with us.

(Anna goes to her house and returns with some carrots, a bowl, and a spoon. Olga returns with a bag of onions.)

167

Olga: Here are some onions. I should like to learn to make this soup.

Anna: Here are the carrots.

Petya: It could use just a bit of potato, too. I cannot say that stone soup is ever quite right without a potato or two.

Olga: That is true. A stone is nothing without a potato!

Marya: If you need some potatoes for that soup of yours, I have a sack in my cottage!

(Marya gets her sack of potatoes from her cottage.)

Marya: Here's a full sack of potatoes.

Petya: Many thanks. Please stay for dinner.

Sasha: These potatoes will really add to the flavor of the soup!

(Sasha dumps the sack of potatoes into the kettle.)

Sergeant: Stop, Sasha. Stop!

Olga: What is the matter, Sergeant?

Sergeant: Sasha has added too many potatoes! The potatoes have absorbed the flavor of the stones.

Villagers: Oh, too bad! What a shame!

Marya: Is there nothing we can do?

Petya: I have an idea. Meat and potatoes go well together. Let's add some meat.

Dmitri: I have a ham. Wait here while I get it.

Sergeant: It might work, at that.

Dmitri: Here's the ham!

Villagers: Good for you, Dmitri! Quick thinking!

Petya: Thank you, Dmitri. I'll put it in myself.

Marya: Can anyone make this stone soup?

Petya: Oh, yes. All you need are stones, fire, water, and hungry people.

Anna: Well, how is it now, soldier? It smells delicious.

Sergeant: Friends, I know this will be a very good soup. You have fine stones in this village, no doubt of that! Stay and eat with us, one and all.

(The villagers get bowls and spoons. The sergeant fills everyone's bowl with soup. Then they begin to eat.)

Dmitri: This is truly a delicious soup, soldiers!

Anna: It has such a hearty flavor!

Marya: It fills you up!

Villagers: This soup is the best we've ever tasted!

Anna: And to think, neighbors, it's made only of stones!

Soldiers: Yes, imagine that! It's made only of stones!

The End

THINK IT OVER

1. What makes the villagers change their minds about sharing with the soldiers?

2. Tell about another way the soldiers could make the villagers share their food.

3. What things do the soldiers use to make the soup?

WRITE

Write the soldiers' recipe for stone soup. Include everything they used and the directions for making the soup.

THE NIGHT OF THE STARS

Douglas Gutiérrez
María Fernandez Oliver

translated by Carmen Diana Dearden

Long, long ago, in a town
that was neither near nor far,
there lived a man

who did not like the night.

During the day, in the sunlight, he worked weaving baskets, watching over his animals and watering his vegetables.

Often he would sing. But as soon as the sun set behind the mountain, this man who did not like the night would become sad, for his world suddenly turned gray, dark and black.

"Night again! Horrible night!" he would cry out.

He would then pick up his baskets, light his lamp and shut himself up in his house.

Sometimes he would look out the window, but there was

nothing to see in the
dark sky.
So he would put out
his lamp and
go to bed.

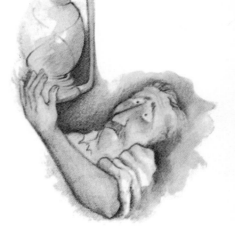

One day, at sunset, the man went to the mountain.
Night was beginning to cover the blue sky.

The man climbed to the highest peak and shouted:

"Please, night. Stop!"

And the night did stop for a moment.

"What is it?" she asked in a soft, deep voice.

"Night, I don't like you. When you come, the light goes
away and the colors disappear. Only the darkness remains."

"You're right," answered the night. "It is so."

"Tell me, where do you take the light?"
asked the man.

"It hides behind me, and I cannot do anything about it,"
replied the night. "I'm very sorry."

The night finished stretching and covered the world
with darkness.

The man came down
    from the mountain
    and went
to bed.

But he could not sleep.

Nor during the next day could he work.

All he could think about was his conversation with the night.

And in the afternoon, when the light began to disappear again, he said to himself: "I know what to do."

Once more he went to the mountain.

The night was like an immense awning, covering all things.

When at last he reached the highest point on the mountain, the man stood on his tiptoes and, with his finger, poked a hole in the black sky.

A pinprick of light flickered through the hole.

The man who did not like the night was delighted.

He poked holes all over the sky. Here, there, everywhere, and all over the sky little points of light appeared.

Amazed now at what he could do, the man made a fist and punched it through the darkness.

A large hole opened up, and a huge, round light, almost like a grapefruit, shone through.

All the escaping light cast a brilliant glow at
the base of the mountain and lit up everything below . . .

the fields, the street, the houses.
Everything.
That night, no one in the town slept.

And ever since then, the night is full of lights,
and people everywhere can stay up late . . .

looking at the moon
and the stars.

THINK IT OVER

1. How does the man feel about night at the beginning of the story and at the end?

2. How do you think the man knows that he should poke holes through the night?

3. What is the large hole that the man makes through the night?

WRITE

Write a few sentences telling what you would do if you could stay up all night.

HELPING HANDS

Do you think that the soldiers have made stone soup before? Why do you think as you do?

. . . .

What do you think the soldiers would cook to help celebrate a night full of lights?

. . . .

WRITER'S WORKSHOP What do you think the soldiers will eat for breakfast the next morning? Think of something you eat for breakfast. Write a few sentences telling how to make it.

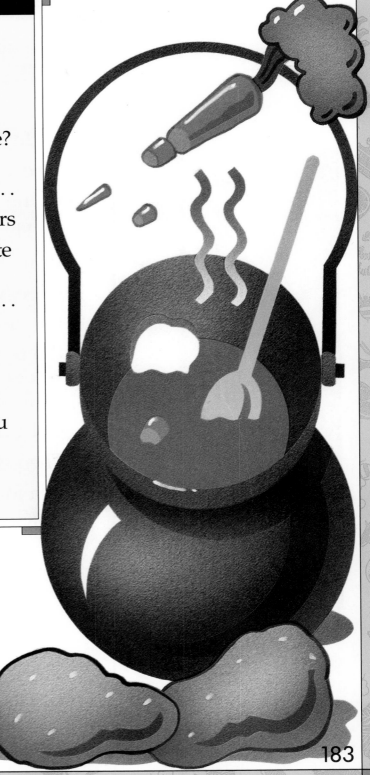

FOOD FESTIVAL

In Japan, every season has its special foods. In winter, families look forward to eating a special hot dish.

First, they pick up chicken meat with their chopsticks. Next, they swish it in a pot of boiling chicken soup. That swishing gives the dish its name—*shabu-shabu*. Finally, they dip the chicken in a spicy sauce.

■ Find out what foods people of other cultures have for special days or seasons. Then work with classmates to draw a mural of a food festival. Show people enjoying dishes from all parts of the world.

FROM TACOS TO TOFU

With a group, plan a menu of healthful foods for a day. Include foods from many parts of the world. Draw a picture of a table set for each meal.

You might use a chart like this one to help you plan.

	Breakfast	Lunch	Dinner
eggs and dairy products			
foods from grains			
fruit and vegetable dishes			
meat or bean dishes			

A TASTE OF THE PAST

Tell about a culture your family is part of. On a map, point out the area where people from your family lived. Then describe a special family dish from that place.

When people work together, they can do wonderful things. Some African American women worked together to make old rags into quilts. The quilts are so beautiful that they hang in museums today. In the next unit, you will read about how people and animals work together to do all sorts of things. You might find an idea for making something with a friend.

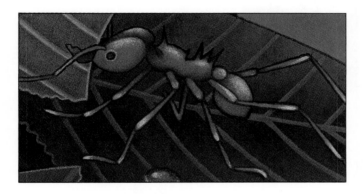

BOOKSHELF

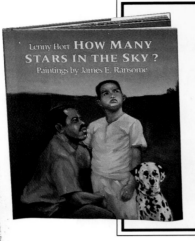

HOW MANY STARS IN THE SKY?
BY LENNY HORT

When a boy and his father can't fall asleep, they go out into the night to count the stars.

HBJ LIBRARY BOOK

ROLLI
BY KOJI TAKIHARA

Rolli, a flower seed, can't remember where he came from and doesn't know where he's going. He just keeps rolling from one adventure to the next. At last he takes root in the soil and grows into a lovely flower.

BACKYARD INSECTS
BY MILLICENT SELSAM

Did you know that there may be more than a thousand different kinds of insects in your back yard? Learn about some of them in this interesting book. AWARD-WINNING AUTHOR

SAM JOHNSON AND THE BLUE RIBBON QUILT
BY LISA CAMPBELL ERNST

Sam Johnson starts mending a torn awning and ends up making a wonderful quilt! But the Rosedale Women's Quilting Club won't let him join their group. So Sam starts a men's quilting club. Which club will make the better quilt? AWARD-WINNING AUTHOR

THE CACTUS FLOWER BAKERY
BY HARRY ALLARD

Sunny the snake is lonely. No one seems to want to be her friend. Then she meets Stewart, a traveling armadillo. Now Sunny has a friend *and* a business partner. AWARD-WINNING BOOK

WORKING HANDS

Have you ever made something special all by yourself? Perhaps you have received a gift that was made by hand. Your gift could have been something to wear, something to play with, or even something to eat. In the next selections, you will read about different things that were made by hand and how they were made.

CONTENTS

THE GOAT IN THE RUG

by Charles L. Blood & Martin Link
illustrated by Nancy Winslow Parker

My name is Geraldine and I live near a place called Window Rock with my Navajo friend, Glenmae. It's called Window Rock because it has a big round hole in it that looks like a window open to the sky.

Glenmae is called Glenmae most of the time because it's easier to say than her Indian name: Glee 'Nasbah. In English that means something like female warrior, but she's really a Navajo weaver. I guess that's why, one day, she decided to weave me into a rug.

I remember it was a warm, sunny afternoon. Glenmae had spent most of the morning sharpening a large pair of scissors. I had no idea what she was going to use them for, but it didn't take me long to find out.

Before I knew what was happening, I was on the ground and Glenmae was clipping off my wool in great long strands. (It's called mohair, really.) It didn't hurt at all, but I admit I kicked up my heels some. I'm very ticklish for a goat.

I might have looked a little naked and silly afterwards, but my, did I feel nice and cool! So I decided to stick around and see what would happen next.

The first thing Glenmae did was chop up roots from a yucca plant. The roots made a soapy, rich lather when she mixed them with water.

She washed my wool in the suds until it was clean and white.

After that, a little bit of me (you might say) was hung up in the sun to dry. When my wool was dry, Glenmae took out two large square combs with many teeth.

By combing my wool between these carding combs, as they're called, she removed any bits of twigs or burrs and straightened out the fibers. She told me it helped make a smoother yarn for spinning.

Then, Glenmae carefully started to spin my wool—one small bundle at a time—into yarn. I was beginning to find out it takes a long while to make a Navajo rug.

Again and again, Glenmae twisted and pulled, twisted and pulled the wool. Then she spun it around a long, thin stick she called a spindle. As she twisted and pulled and spun, the finer, stronger and smoother the yarn became.

A few days later, Glenmae and I went for a walk. She said we were going to find some special plants she would use to make dye.

I didn't know what "dye" meant, but it sounded like a picnic to me. I do love to eat plants. That's what got me into trouble.

While Glenmae was out looking for more plants, I ate every one she had already collected in her bucket. Delicious!

The next day, Glenmae made me stay home while she walked miles to a store. She said the dye she could buy wasn't the same as the kind she makes from plants, but since I'd made such a pig of myself, it would have to do.

I was really worried that she would still be angry with me when she got back. She wasn't, though, and pretty soon she had three big potfuls of dye boiling over a fire.

Then I saw what Glenmae had meant by dyeing. She dipped my white wool into one pot . . . and it turned pink! She dipped it in again. It turned a darker pink! By the time she'd finished dipping it in and out and hung it up to dry, it was a beautiful deep red.

After that, she dyed some of my wool brown, and some of it black. I couldn't help wondering if those plants I'd eaten would turn all of me the same colors.

While I was worrying about that, Glenmae started to make our rug. She took a ball of yarn and wrapped it around and around two poles. I lost count when she'd reached three hundred wraps. I guess I was too busy thinking about what it would be like to be the only red, white, black and brown goat at Window Rock.

It wasn't long before Glenmae had finished wrapping. Then she hung the poles with the yarn on a big wooden frame. It looked like a picture frame made of logs—she called it a "loom."

After a whole week of getting ready to weave, Glenmae started. She began weaving at the bottom of the loom. Then, one strand of yarn at a time, our rug started growing toward the top.

A few strands of black.

A few of brown.

A few of red.

In and out. Back and forth.

Until, in a few days, the pattern of our rug was clear to see.

Our rug grew very slowly. Just as every Navajo weaver before her had done for hundreds and hundreds of years, Glenmae formed a design that would never be duplicated.

Then, at last, the weaving was finished! But not until I'd checked it quite thoroughly in front . . .

. . . and in back, did I let Glenmae take our rug off the loom.

There was a lot of me in that rug. I wanted it to be perfect. And it was.

Since then, my wool has grown almost long enough for Glenmae and me to make another rug. I hope we do very soon. Because, you see, there aren't too many weavers like Glenmae left among the Navajos.

And there's only one goat like me, Geraldine.

THINK IT OVER

1. What does Geraldine mean when she says, "There was a lot of me in that rug"?

2. What colors does Glenmae dye the wool?

3. Do you have a favorite toy or piece of clothing that was made by hand? Tell about it.

WRITE

What does Glenmae do to make the wool ready for weaving? Write a list of the things she does to the wool.

ONE HAT, COMING UP!

BIG BROTHERS ARE SUPPOSED TO TEACH THEIR YOUNGER SISTERS HOW TO MAKE THINGS..

OKAY, WHAT DO YOU WANT TO MAKE?

SHOW ME HOW TO MAKE A HAT OUT OF A NEWSPAPER...

8-14

Thunder cake

by PATRICIA POLACCO

On sultry summer days at my grandma's farm in Michigan, the air gets damp and heavy. Stormclouds drift low over the fields. Birds fly close to the ground. The clouds glow for an instant with a sharp, crackling light, and then a roaring, low, tumbling sound of thunder makes the windows shudder in their panes. The sound used to scare me when I was little. I loved to go to Grandma's house (Babushka, as I used to call my grandma, had come from Russia years before), but I feared Michigan's summer storms. I feared the sound of thunder more than anything. I always hid under the bed when the storm moved near the farmhouse.

This is the story of how my grandma— my Babushka—helped me overcome my fear of thunderstorms.

Grandma looked at the horizon, drew a deep breath and said, "This is Thunder Cake baking weather, all right. Looks like a storm coming to me."

"Child, you come out from under that bed. It's only thunder you're hearing," my grandma said.

The air was hot, heavy and damp. A loud clap of thunder shook the house, rattled the windows and made me grab her close.

"Steady, child," she cooed. "Unless you let go of me, we won't be able to make a Thunder Cake today!"

"Thunder Cake?" I stammered as I hugged her even closer.

"Don't pay attention to that old thunder, except to see how close the storm is getting. When you see the lightning, start counting . . . real slow. When you hear the thunder, stop counting. That number is how many miles away the storm is. Understand?" she asked. "We need to know how far away the storm is, so we have time to make the cake and get it into the oven before the storm comes, or it won't be real Thunder Cake."

Her eyes surveyed the black clouds a way off in the distance. Then she strode into the kitchen. Her worn hands pulled a thick book from the shelf above the woodstove.

"Let's find that recipe, child," she crowed as she lovingly fingered the grease-stained pages to a creased spot.

"Here it is . . . Thunder Cake!"

She carefully penned the ingredients on a piece of notepaper. "Now let's gather all the things we'll need!" she exclaimed as she scurried toward the back door.

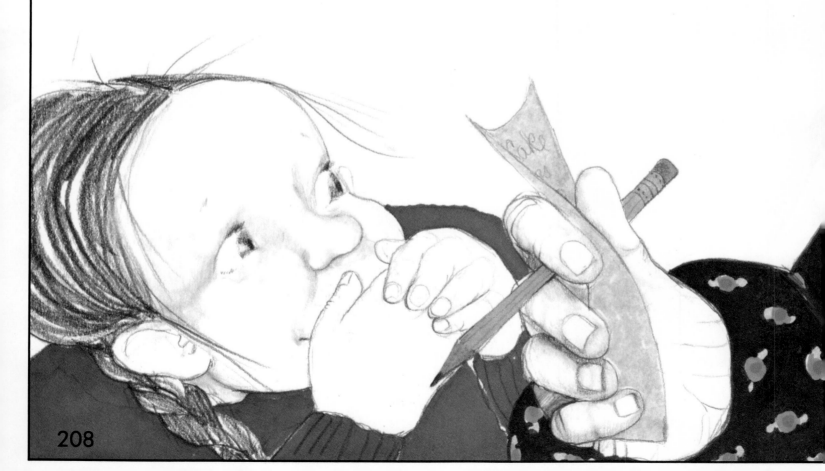

We were by the barn door when a huge bolt of
lightning flashed. I started counting, like Grandma told
me to, "1–2–3–4–5–6–7–8–9–10."

Then the thunder ROARED!

"Ten miles . . . it's ten miles away," Grandma said as
she looked at the sky. "About an hour away, I'd say. You'll
have to hurry, child. Gather them eggs careful-like," she
said.

Eggs from mean old Nellie Peck Hen. I was scared. I
knew she would try to peck me.

"I'm here, she won't hurt you. Just get them eggs,"
Grandma said softly.

The lightning flashed again. "1–2–3–4–5–6–7–8–9"
I counted. "Nine miles," Grandma reminded me.

Milk was next. Milk from old Kick Cow. As
Grandma milked her, Kick Cow turned and looked
mean, right at me. I was scared. She looked so big.

ZIP went the lightning. "1–2–3–4–5–6–7–8" I
counted.

BAROOOOOOOOM went the thunder.

"Eight miles, child," Grandma croaked. "Now we have
to get chocolate and sugar and flour from the dry shed."

I was scared as we walked down the path from the farmhouse through Tangleweed Woods to the dry shed. Suddenly the lightning slit the sky!

"1–2–3–4–5–6–7" I counted.

BOOOOOOM BA-BOOOOOOM, crashed the thunder. It scared me a lot, but I kept walking with Grandma.

Another jagged edge of lightning flashed as I crept into the dry shed! "1–2–3–4–5–6" I counted.

CRACKLE, CRACKLE BOOOOOOOM, KA-BOOOOOM, the thunder bellowed. It was dark and I was scared.

"I'm here, child," Grandma said softly from the doorway. "Hurry now, we haven't got much time. We've got everything but the secret ingredient."

"Three overripe tomatoes and some strawberries,"
Grandma whispered as she squinted at the list.

I climbed up high on the trellis. The ground looked a
long way down. I was scared.

"I'm here, child," she said. Her voice was steady and
soft. "You won't fall."

I reached three luscious tomatoes while she picked
strawberries. Lightning again! "1–2–3–4–5" I counted.

KA-BANG BOOOOOOOOOAROOOOM, the
thunder growled.

We hurried back to the house and the warm kitchen, and we measured the ingredients. I poured them into the mixing bowl while Grandma mixed. I churned butter for the frosting and melted chocolate. Finally, we poured the batter into the cake pans and put them into the oven together.

Lightning lit the kitchen! I only counted to three and the thunder RRRRUMBLED and CRASHED.

"Three miles away," Grandma said, "and the cake is in the oven. We made it! We'll have a real Thunder Cake!"

As we waited for the cake, Grandma looked out the window for a long time. "Why, you aren't afraid of thunder. You're too brave!" she said as she looked right at me.

"I'm not brave, Grandma," I said. "I was under the bed! Remember?"

"But you got out from under it," she answered, "and you got eggs from mean old Nellie Peck Hen, you got milk from old Kick Cow, you went through Tangleweed Woods to the dry shed, you climbed the trellis in the barnyard. From where I sit, only a very brave person could have done all them things!"

I thought and thought as the storm rumbled closer. She was right. I was brave!

"Brave people can't be afraid of a sound, child," she said as we spread out the tablecloth and set the table. When we were done, we hurried into the kitchen to take the cake out of the oven. After the cake had cooled, we frosted it.

Just then the lightning flashed, and this time it lit the whole sky.

Even before the last flash had faded, the thunder ROLLED, BOOOOOMED, CRASHED, and BBBBAAAAARRRRROOOOOOOOMMMMMMMM-MMED just above us. The storm was here!

"Perfect," Grandma cooed, "just perfect." She beamed as she added the last strawberry to the glistening chocolate frosting on top of our Thunder Cake.

As rain poured down on our roof, Grandma cut a wedge for each of us. She poured us steaming cups of tea from the samovar.

When the thunder ROARED above us so hard it shook the windows and rattled the dishes in the cupboards, we just smiled and ate our Thunder Cake.

From that time on, I never feared the voice of thunder again.

My Grandma's Thunder Cake

Cream together, one at a time

    1 cup shortening
    1 3/4 cup sugar
    1 teaspoon vanilla
    3 eggs, separated
        (Blend yolks in. Beat whites
        until they are stiff, then
        fold in.)

1 cup cold water
1/3 cup pureed tomatoes

Sift together

    2 1/2 cups cake flour
    1/2 cup dry cocoa
    1 1/2 teaspoons baking soda
    1 teaspoon salt

Mix dry mixture into creamy mixture. Bake in two greased and floured 8 1/2-inch round pans at 350° for 35 to 40 minutes. Frost with chocolate butter frosting. Top with strawberries.

THINK IT OVER

1. How does Grandma help the girl overcome her fear of thunderstorms?
2. What are the secret ingredients that Grandma puts into the Thunder Cake?
3. Why does Grandma say the girl is brave?

WRITE

Think about something you helped make. Draw a picture of what you made, and write some sentences about it.

My CREATURE

by **Jack Prelutsky**

picture by **Marylin Hafner**

I made a creature
out of clay,
just what it is
is hard to say.
Its neck is thin,
its legs are fat,
it's like a bear
and like a bat.
It's like a snake
and like a snail,
it has a little curly tail,
a shaggy mane,
a droopy beard,
its ears are long,
its smile is weird.

It has four horns,
one beady eye,
two floppy wings
(though it can't fly),
it only sits
upon my shelf—
just think, I made it
by myself!

Jack Prelutsky

AWARD-WINNING
AUTHOR

Ms. Cooper, a writer, asked Jack Prelutsky some questions about himself.

Cooper: Where did you get the idea for "My Creature"?

Prelutsky: When I was a kid, and the teacher said, "Draw a bird," everyone would draw a regular bird. But I'd say, "Hey, what if the bird had a horn?" So my creatures never looked like anyone else's. After a while I decided I liked my own creatures better.

Cooper: When did you start to write poetry?

Prelutsky: My writing came out of my drawing. I was trying to sell a book about imaginary creatures, so I had drawn lots of pictures to show the publisher. When I finished the drawings, I decided they needed poems to go along with them. The publisher didn't want my artwork, but she loved the poems.

Cooper: What do you do when you're not writing?

Prelutsky: I read a lot, I make funny little sculptures out of plastic, and I garden. I'm also inventing my own computer games.

WORKING HANDS

Why are Geraldine the goat and the girl in "Thunder Cake" happy with what they helped make?

. . . .

The girl in the poem "My Creature" describes the creature that she makes. How do you think Geraldine would describe the rug that she helps make? Make the description rhyme if you can.

. . . .

WRITER'S WORKSHOP Think of something you know how to make. Then write down directions telling how to make it. Have a friend try to make it by using your instructions.

INSECTS AT WORK

Have you ever watched ants or other insects getting food? Did you know that ants live and work together in ant cities? In the following selections, you will learn more about ants and other insects.

C O N T E N T S

ANTS LIVE HERE

Ants live here
by the curb stone,
    see?
They worry a lot
about giants like
    me.

Lilian Moore

UNDER THE GROUND

What is under the grass,
Way down in the ground,
Where everything is cool and wet
With darkness all around?

Little pink worms live there;
Ants and brown bugs creep
Softly round the stones and rocks
Where roots are pushing deep.

Do they hear us walking
On the grass above their heads;
Hear us running over
While they snuggle in their beds?

Rhoda W. Bacmeister

BUG POEMS

THE UNDERWORLD

When I am lying in the grass
I watch the ants and beetles pass;
And once I lay so very still
A mole beside me built a hill.

Margaret Lavington

ANTS

I like to watch the ants at work
When I am out at play.
I like to see them run about
And carry crumbs away.

And when I plug an anthill door
To keep them in their den,
I like to see them find a way
To get outside again.

Mary Ann Hoberman

Illustrations by Jennifer Hewitson

227

ANT CITIES

WRITTEN AND ILLUSTRATED BY ARTHUR DORROS

OUTSTANDING
SCIENCE TRADE
BOOK

When it is sunny,
the top of the nest
gets warm.

When it rains, water
runs off the hill.

If it gets too wet
near the top of the nest,
the ants move below.

In winter the ants hibernate in a deep room away from the cold. They stay together in a ball to keep warm.

Have you seen ants busy running over a hill of dirt? They may look like they are just running around. But the ants built that hill to live in, and each ant has work to do.

Some ants may disappear into a small hole in the hill. The hole is the door to their nest.

These are harvester ants. Their nest is made of lots of rooms and tunnels. These little insects made them all.

Underneath the hill there may be miles of tunnels and hundreds of rooms. The floors are worn smooth by thousands of ant feet. It is dark inside the nest. But the ants stay cozy.

In the rooms of the nest, worker ants do many different kinds of work. It is like a city, a busy city of ants.

Some ants have brought in food to the ant city. These harvester ants like seeds.

A worker ant cracks the husks off the seeds. Another worker will take the husks outside to throw away.

The ants chew the seeds to get the juices out. Then they feed the juices to the other ants.

Other workers store seeds for the ants to eat another time.

Not all ants store food. But harvester ants do.

In one room of the nest, a queen ant lays eggs. Workers carry the eggs away to other rooms to take care of them.

Each ant city has to have at least one queen. Without a queen there would be no ant city. All the other ants in the ant city grow from the eggs the queen lays.

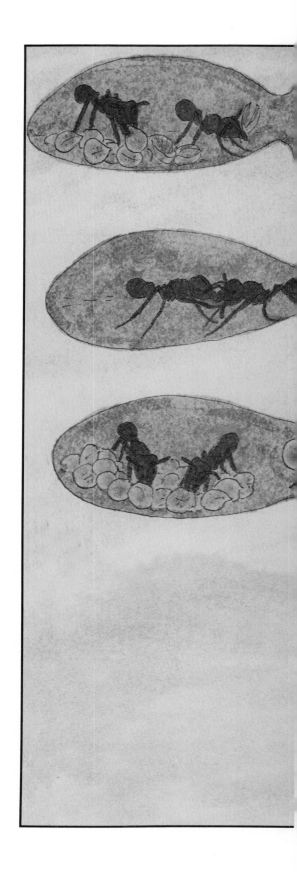

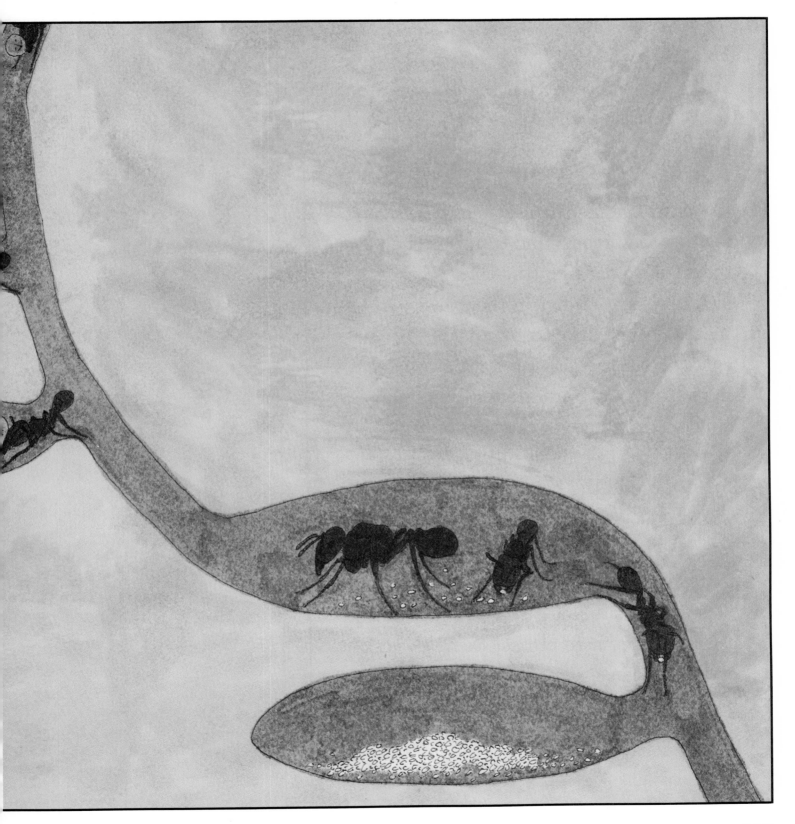

The queen doesn't tell the workers what to do. But the workers are busy. Each ant has work to do. Ants work together to keep the whole ant city alive.

Workers make the nest bigger by digging new rooms and tunnels. They use their feet to dig like tiny dogs. Workers pick up pieces of dirt in their jaws and "beards" and carry them outside.

Dirt from the digging is what makes the anthill. Ants are great diggers and builders. Imagine all the tiny pieces of dirt it takes to build a hill two feet high.

Out around the harvester anthill, workers look for food. Harvester ants mostly eat seeds. But sometimes they eat insects, too.

Ants can bite and sting other insects to capture them or to protect themselves. Be careful, because some kinds of ants can bite or sting you, too. Harvester ants will bite or sting if you disturb their nest.

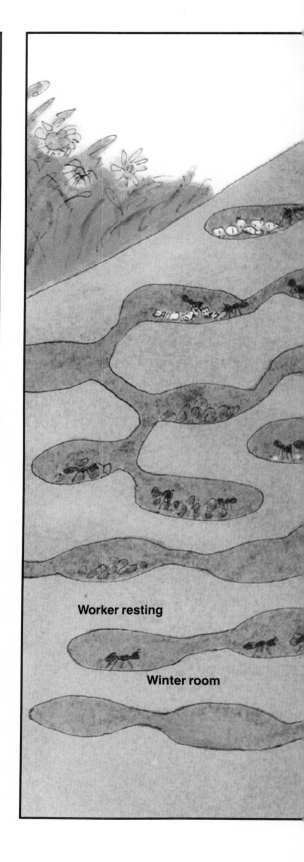

Worker resting

Winter room

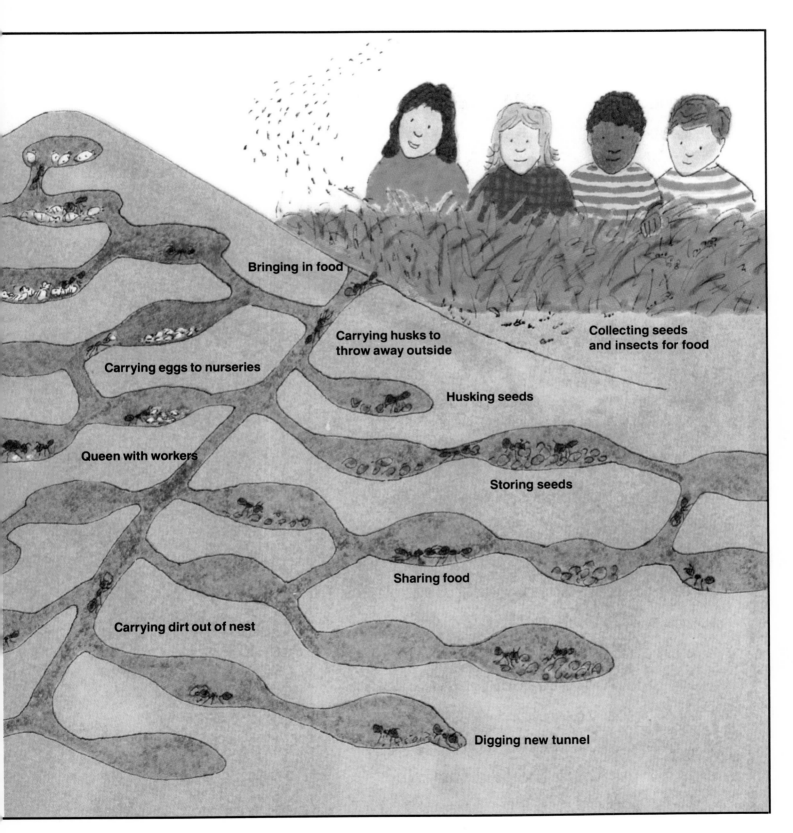

Bringing in food

Carrying husks to
throw away outside

Collecting seeds
and insects for food

Carrying eggs to nurseries

Husking seeds

Queen with workers

Storing seeds

Sharing food

Carrying dirt out of nest

Digging new tunnel

Ants use their antennas to help them find food. They touch and smell with their antennas.

Antennas

**Comb
on legs for
cleaning antennas**

If one ant finds food, others follow. Soon there will be a lot of ants carrying away lunch.

If one ant can't carry something, others may help. But each worker ant is strong. An ant can lift as much as fifty times its own weight. If people could lift like that, we could each lift a car.

The workers carry the food back to the ant city. Ants share the food they find.

Ants eat many foods.
But different kinds of ants
like different foods.
There are over 10,000
kinds of ants.

Formica ants mostly eat
juices that they suck from
insects they kill.

Cornfield ants like to eat
the sweet juices, or
"honeydew," they get
from aphids. Aphids
suck the juices from
plants. Then the ants
"milk" the aphids for
honeydew.

Carpenter ants especially
like sweet juices they can
get from insects, and from
plants, too.

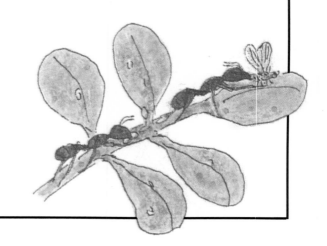

Thief ants eat sweets and other food they find in people's houses and lying about.

Leaf-cutting ants (parasol ants) make underground gardens with leaves they cut. They grow mushrooms in the gardens for food.

Army ants travel in large groups like armies. They devour huge numbers of insects, including termites.

The different kinds of ants have found many ways to make their cities, so they can live in many kinds of places.

Janitor ants make their nests in hollowed-out tree twigs. The soldier janitor ant—a kind of worker ant—has a big, plug-shaped head it can use for a door.

Many kinds of ants make hills or mounds. If you haven't seen harvester anthills, maybe you've seen the round-topped hills that formica ants make. Sometimes they cover their hills with thatch.

Formica ant

238

Pavement ants are tiny ants—1/8 inch long.
Harvester ants are about 1/4 inch long.
Some ants are as big as 2 inches long.

Or you may have seen pavement ants. They can live under the sidewalk.

Or carpenter ants, who build their nests in rotting wood.

There are small ant cities with just a few ants. There are big ant cities with many, many ants. Ants have been found at the tops of the highest buildings and on ships at sea.

Ants can make their cities almost anywhere. Look around and you'll probably find an ant city, busy with ants.

THINK IT OVER

1. How is the ants' nest like a city?

2. What are the jobs of the ants that live together in the anthill?

3. If you were as strong as a worker ant, what would you be able to do?

WRITE

What kind of ants might build a home in your neighborhood? Write the reasons for your choice.

INSECTS AT WORK

Do you think that ants always work and never play? What do you think a city of ants would do for fun?

. . . .

Which underground creature is your favorite? Tell why.

. . . .

WRITER'S WORKSHOP Imagine that you are an ant or other small insect. Write a poem telling how you feel living close to people and other "giants." Share your poem with a classmate.

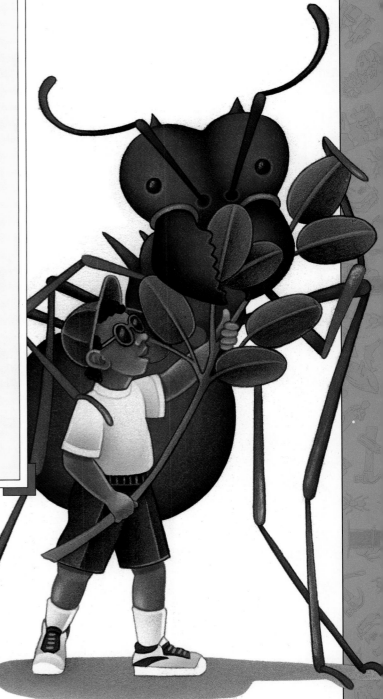

HELPING THE ENVIRONMENT

Do you worry about the environment? Perhaps you recycle bottles and cans. Perhaps you care about saving animals. In the next selections, you will read about a hurt whale and about how you can help make the world a better place.

C O N T E N T S

IBIS
A True Whale Story
by John Himmelman

AWARD-WINNING
AUTHOR

 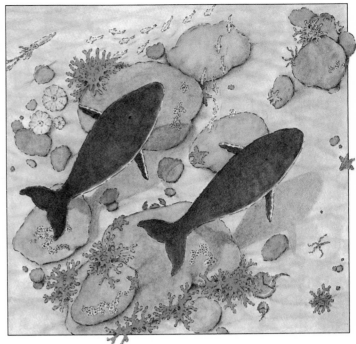

Deep in a bay, off the coast of an old fishing village, lived a pod of humpback whales.

One of the whales was a little calf named Ibis. Ibis was curious about everything in the ocean.

One day she and her friend Blizzard went out swimming. They saw many kinds of fish. The most interesting were the starfish. Ibis liked to look at them. There was something about their shape that made her feel good.

As Ibis and Blizzard were drifting over a reef they heard a strange humming noise. The two calves looked up to see something large and dark pass overhead. It was as big as a whale, but it wasn't a whale.

The calves were frightened. They had never seen a boat before. They swam back to their mothers.

The next day, Ibis went back to the reef. It wasn't long before another boat came along. Again, Ibis was scared. But she was curious, too. She forced herself to swim to the surface.

In the cool, hazy air, she saw several faces watching her. They didn't look scary. In fact, they looked very friendly. Ibis liked them.

In the months that followed, Ibis and her friends lost their fear of boats. Boats came in many sizes and shapes, and the people in them always seemed to enjoy seeing the little whales.

As Ibis grew up, she learned more about the sea. She knew what kinds of sharks to avoid, what food was the tastiest, and, best of all, where to find the most dazzling starfish. Ibis never got tired of looking at starfish.

People and their boats became a part of her life. Whenever a boat passed overhead, she swam to the top to say hello.

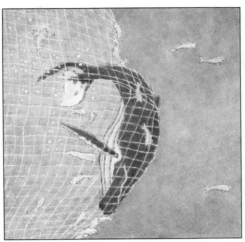

One evening, Ibis and Blizzard saw a school of fish swimming around the bottom of a ship.

Maybe there was something good up there to eat. They went to find out.

Suddenly Ibis was caught in a fishing net! She fought to get free. But the more she struggled, the more tangled up she became.

Finally she broke loose, but part of the net was caught in her mouth and wrapped around her tail.

Blizzard swam off to find help.

Ibis was confused and hurt. She wanted to get away, far from people and their boats and nets. Slowly and painfully she made her way toward the deep ocean.

Many weeks passed, and Ibis grew very ill. The net in her mouth made it hard for her to eat. And every time she went to the surface for air, the net cut into her tail. But if she didn't get air every half hour, she would die.

Winter was coming, and it was time for the whales to move to warmer waters. But Ibis felt too weak to make the long journey.

Instead she turned back toward the coast. It was so hard for her to swim, she could barely keep moving. Ibis was about to give up. Then she saw a familiar shape. It was Blizzard!

Blizzard saw that Ibis needed help. Gently Blizzard pushed her to the surface so she could breathe.

Suddenly the water was filled with the sounds of boat engines. The whales saw two small rafts and a boat circling them.

Blizzard and Ibis tried to get away fast. But Ibis wasn't quick enough. The boats rushed toward her before she could dive.

The people in the boats began to attach large floats to the pieces of net that were hurting Ibis. Blizzard stayed nearby, circling the boats nervously.

Because of the floats, Ibis could not dive. She began to panic, but she did not have the strength to fight. When the boats came in closer, a person reached into the water.

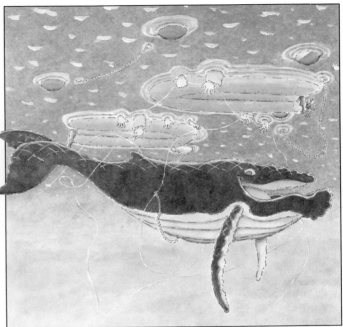

Ibis stared at the person's hand. The hand reminded her of something—something she loved very much. She began to feel better.

Soon many hands dipped into the water. Ibis felt them tugging at the lines of the net. Moments later the lines fell away, and she was free!

Ibis blew a big spout from her blowhole as if to say, "Thank you! Thank you!" Then she dived deep into the water. For the first time in many weeks, she felt no pain. She felt wonderful!

Blizzard joined her. Then the two whales popped back to the surface for one more look.

The people were waving their starfish-shaped hands.
Ibis knew the hands had helped her, and that the people
were still her friends.

Soon Blizzard and Ibis were leaping and diving with the other whales, far away in the warm waters where they would spend the winter together.

THINK IT OVER

1. What do you think makes Ibis a special whale?

2. What happens after Ibis gets caught in the net?

3. Why does Ibis feel better when she sees the person's hand in the water?

4. What can you do to keep the area where you live safe for the animals that live there too?

WRITE

Imagine that you were on the boat that rescued Ibis. Write a letter to the captain of the fishing boat that threw the net, telling about Ibis.

Let's Help Save the Earth

from **How Green Are You?**
written by David Bellamy
illustrated by Lynne Cherry

How the whale can help us

Only 400 years ago, there were many whales of all kinds. They had few enemies until people started hunting them. Then so many whales were killed that some kinds nearly became extinct.

In the last 20 years people have persuaded most governments around the world to stop the killing of whales— and now the number of whales is beginning to grow again.

The Friendly Whale says thank you for helping to save the whales. Now she is going to help us save ourselves. The letters **W, H, A, L** and **E** stand for **W**ater, **H**abitat, **A**ir, **L**ife and **E**nergy— the five most important parts of our environment. Each of these is in danger.

Water

We need clean water to drink, to cook with and to wash with. When we have finished with it, we throw it away. Every day lots of dirt and chemicals pour into the rivers and seas from our homes, factories and farms. We use so much water that there is often not enough to go around.

The Friendly Whale says look for this symbol to see how you can save water and make your waste water cleaner.

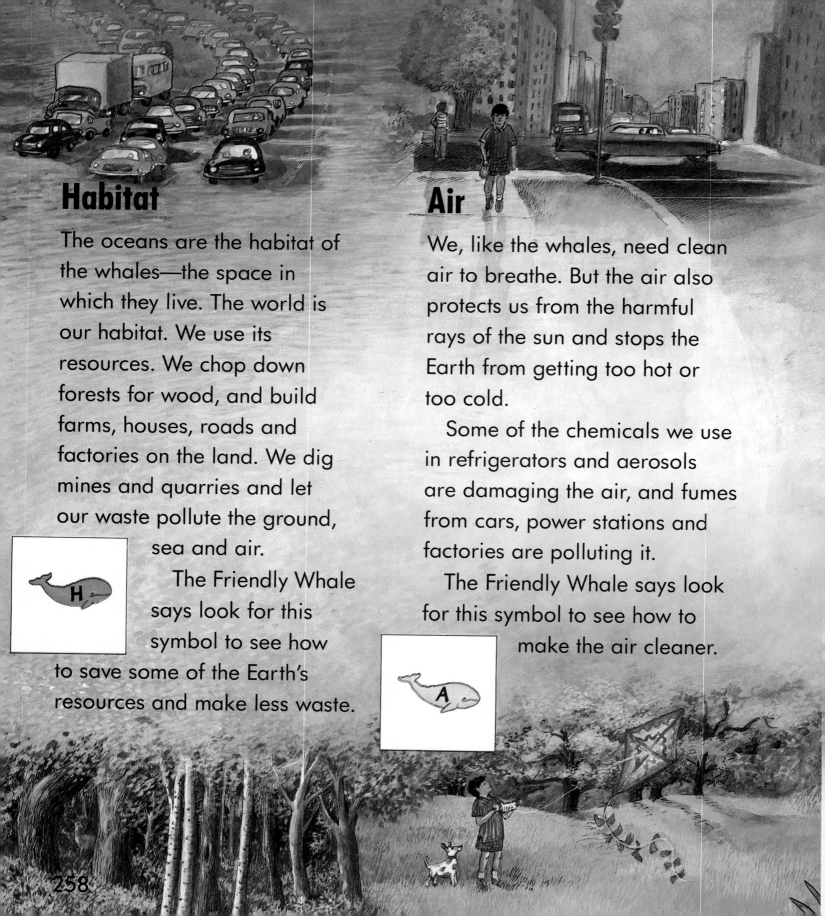

Habitat

The oceans are the habitat of the whales—the space in which they live. The world is our habitat. We use its resources. We chop down forests for wood, and build farms, houses, roads and factories on the land. We dig mines and quarries and let our waste pollute the ground, sea and air.

The Friendly Whale says look for this symbol to see how to save some of the Earth's resources and make less waste.

Air

We, like the whales, need clean air to breathe. But the air also protects us from the harmful rays of the sun and stops the Earth from getting too hot or too cold.

Some of the chemicals we use in refrigerators and aerosols are damaging the air, and fumes from cars, power stations and factories are polluting it.

The Friendly Whale says look for this symbol to see how to make the air cleaner.

Life

We have helped to save the whales from extinction, but every day more than 10 sorts of plants and animals become extinct. By the year 2000 more than a million kinds of plants and animals may have been wiped out. Most of these plants and animals come from the huge rainforests that grow near the equator.

The Friendly Whale says look for this symbol and do what you can to help plants and animals.

Energy

Energy is what makes things work. The food you eat gives you energy to run and jump. Cars and trucks burn gasoline or oil to make them go. Stoves, heaters and many other things use the energy of gas, or electricity, which is made by burning oil or coal. We get oil, coal and gas from deep under the ground, but soon there will be none left.

The Friendly Whale says look for this symbol to see how to save energy.

259

In the bathroom

How much dirty water do you pour down the drains every day? It is not only the dirt but the soap and chemical cleaners too that spoil the water.

The Friendly Whale shows how you and your family can use less water and keep clean without harming the environment too much.

Make sure your shampoos, hair conditioners, creams and lotions have not been tested on animals. Make especially sure they do not contain whale oil.

Save water by taking a shower instead of a bath. This saves energy too, because you'll use less hot water and won't use so much electricity, gas or oil.

Save water! Ask your parents to put a brick in the tank so that you won't flush so much water down the toilet each time.

What is biodegradable?

Trees are litterbugs, dropping millions of leaves every autumn. But their litter is biodegradable. The leaves rot and slowly disappear into the soil, making it rich and healthy. Many chemical cleaners and plastics do not rot, because they are not biodegradable. Instead they stay in the soil or water and can poison it.

In the kitchen

You may not think that what you do inside your home can affect the air high in the sky, up to 13 miles above your head, but it does. When power stations burn oil or coal to make your electricity, tons of smoke pour from their chimneys and pollute the air. The Friendly Whale shows how you can help to save electricity and make the air cleaner.

Ask your parents to use biodegradable dishwashing products.

Make sure your dishwasher is fully loaded before using it. Better still, wash dishes by hand. Save water by using a bowl or sink plug.

Make sure all your aerosols are ozone-friendly.

Make sure your take-out food is packed in ozone-friendly boxes. Ask before you buy!

What is ozone-friendly?

There is a layer of ozone gas 13 miles above the Earth. It stops most of the sun's harmful rays from reaching us. But recently the ozone layer has become much thinner in places and has large holes in it. We know that chemicals called CFCs, which we use in refrigerators, aerosols and some foam packing, can destroy ozone. Ozone-friendly aerosols and packing do not contain CFCs.

263

What's in the trash can?

We throw away huge amounts of garbage every day. People in poorer countries cannot afford to waste anything. They mend and use again whatever they can. The Friendly Whale shows how we too can re-use or recycle much of the rubbish in our trash cans.

Save plastic bags to use again for shopping or for lining waste baskets. Most plastic is made from oil, so when you save it you save oil.

Save aluminum and tin cans to be recycled. Use a magnet to tell them apart—tin cans stick, aluminum ones do not. It you re-use metals, you take less from the Earth.

Save old newspapers to be recycled. Paper is made from trees, so when you save it you save trees and forests too.

Save glass jars and bottles and take them to a recycling center.

What is recycling?

Paper is made from trees. Cans are made from metal. Plastic and acrylic materials are made from oil. Every time new things are manufactured they use more of the Earth's resources. But paper and rags can be recycled to make more paper, and cans can be made into new blocks of metal.

RECYCLE

RECYCLED PAPER

THINK IT OVER

1. Why is it important that we all work to save the earth?

2. What five parts of the environment need our help?

3. How will recycling help the environment?

WRITE

Write down at least three things you and your family can start doing to save the earth. Put up your list at home.

265

On My Pond

Words and Music by Kermit the Frog
with Sarah Durkee and Christopher Cerf
Illustrations by Tom Cooke

There's a place where I can sit,
    just me, myself and I . . .
On my pond,
On my pond.

Where the water's fresh and clean
    and peaceful as a sigh . . .
On my pond,
On my pond.

Look at the grass all around me,
It's green as the smile on my face,
Look at the trees, they astound me!
Wow, what a byoo-tiful plaaace!

There's a spot where no one lives
    but quiet little fish . . .
On my pond,
On my pond.

Nature lets me come and visit
   any time I wish . . .
On my pond,
On my pond.

Look at us ALL, . . .
   we're enjoying
A breath of sweet country air . . .
Hey, this is getting ANNOYING!
PLEASE KEEP IT DOWN OVER THEEEERE . . . !

WAIT A MINUTE, WHO SAID YOU COULD
   DUMP YOUR GARBAGE HERE? . . .
On my pond,
On my pond.

267

CLEANIN' IT ALL UP AGAIN
   COULD TAKE US YEARS AND YEARS . . .
On my pond,
On my pond.

Keepin' it clean to BEGIN WITH!
Yes, that's the smart thing to do!
   Don't let 'em cover our fins with
   Any more black slimy gooooo . . . !

Save a place where I can sit,
   just me, myself and I . . .
On my pond,
On my pond.

Keep the water fresh and clean
   and peaceful as a sigh . . .
On my pond,
On my pond!

HELPING THE ENVIRONMENT

How do the people who save Ibis help the environment?

· ·

Ibis and Kermit both live in water. How can you help keep Ibis, Kermit, and other water creatures safe?

· ·

WRITER'S WORKSHOP How can you make the earth a better place to live? Make a poster showing a problem you want to solve and how you would solve it. Share your poster with your classmates.

CONNECTIONS

CLASS QUILT

In the past, very little was thrown away. Clothes were worn until they were almost rags. The rags were then used to make warm and handsome quilts.

African American women made many of these quilts. Some of these women were artists who broke the old rules of quilt-making by making new patterns. Today some of their quilts are found in museums.

■ Quilts often tell a story about the quilt-makers. Make a class quilt out of paper. Draw one square that tells a story about you. Then tape your square to your classmates' squares to form a quilt. Take turns telling about your own quilt square.

GIFTS FROM THROWAWAYS

With a group, list things that people throw away. Then think of useful gifts that might be made from each of the things. Choose one of the gift ideas and write directions for how to make it.

You can use a chart like this to record your ideas.

Things that are thrown away	What they could be made into
egg cartons	
tin cans	
shoe boxes	
plastic bottles	

RECYCLED ART

Create a work of art with things that have been thrown away. You might glue what you find to cardboard, stick it into clay, or hang it from strings.

HANDBOOK
FOR
READERS AND WRITERS

ACTIVE READING STRATEGIES

When you are shooting baskets or making cookies, people sometimes give you ideas that help you. These ideas are called strategies. Using strategies can help you do things better. There are strategies for doing many things, even for reading!

Felipe uses strategies to become a better reader. He asks himself questions before he reads, during his reading and after he reads. Here is how he does this.

Before reading, Felipe uses these strategies.

- ✓ First, I **preview** the story by quickly looking through it.

  What is it about? What is in the pictures?

- ✓ Next, I see whether I already know anything about this story.

  Does this remind me of anything I know or anything I've done?

- ✓ Then, I **predict** what will happen in the story.

  What will happen? What will I learn?

- ✓ Now, I think about my **purpose** for reading. I decide why I want to read this story.

  Will this be fun to read? Am I reading to learn something?

During reading, Felipe stops once in a while to ask himself questions.

✓ I need to make sure I'm reading well.

Do I understand what's happening? Would making a list or a chart help?

✓ I'll see if this book is what I expected it to be.

Do my predictions match what I'm reading? Am I learning what I thought I would? Should I make some different predictions?

✓ This is a word I don't know.

Can I understand the sentence without knowing the word?

Can I figure out the word by checking the sounds its letters stand for? Will the words around it help tell me what it means?

After reading, Felipe thinks about what he has read.

✓ I think about my predictions.

> *How was the book the same as I expected? How was it different?*

✓ I think about my purpose for reading.

> *Did I like the story? Did I learn what I thought I would?*

READING FICTION

Fiction is writing that authors make up. All fiction is make-believe, even though some fiction seems real. Fiction is often fun to read. Some strategies can make reading it even more fun.

The words beside the story on the next two pages show you how Chiang uses strategies **before** and **during** her reading of "Awful Aardvark."

- Before Chiang reads, she previews the story. She predicts what will happen from the title and the pictures.
- She thinks about what she already knows and sets a purpose for reading.

Most of the pictures are of animals. Aardvark has a long nose and long ears that stand up. He sleeps in a tree. He doesn't look awful. I want to read to find out why Aardvark is called Awful.

Aardvark is very strange-looking. The other animals don't seem happy. I think Aardvark does something to make the other animals angry.

■ During her reading, Chiang stops to make sure she understands what she is reading and to check her predictions.

It looks as if Mongoose is not happy with Aardvark's snoring. I think he's angry. I wonder what his idea is.

Awful Aardvark

by Mwalimu

Aardvark was asleep in his favorite tree. The tree was old and dry, but it had a smooth branch where Aardvark would lie and rest his long nose.

And what a nose! His snoring was so loud that it kept Mongoose and all the other animals awake night after night. HHHRRR—ZZZZ! went Aardvark's nose.

"How awful," Mongoose yawned. "I wish he would keep quiet or go somewhere else."

Aardvark only stopped snoring when the sun came up. Then he clambered to the ground and set off to hunt for tasty grubs and crunchy beetles.

While Aardvark was hunting for breakfast, Mongoose had an idea. "I will just have to annoy him more than he annoys me," he decided.

First Mongoose had a meeting with the Monkeys. Next he went to see Lion. Then he talked to Rhinoceros.

That night, as usual, Aardvark climbed up to his branch in the tree and very soon he was snoring HHHRRR—ZZZZ!

Mongoose called into the darkness. The Monkeys came, and the tree shook as they chattered and screeched in the branches.

Aardvark woke up. "Stop making that noise," he shouted. But he soon went back to sleep and snored even more loudly than before. HHHRRR—ZZZZ!

Then Mongoose called out again. There was a low, rumbling growl as Lion came pad-pad-padding to the tree where Aardvark was snoring.

Stretching his legs and reaching high, Lion SCRAAATCHED the bark with his strong claws.

Aardvark woke up again. "Stop it! Go away!" he shouted. But soon he was snoring again, louder than ever. HHHRRR—ZZZZ!

■ Chiang draws a conclusion about Aardvark's snoring and makes another prediction.

Mongoose's plan with the Monkeys didn't work. I think Lion will be able to help.

What is this word? What sounds do the letters stand for? It starts like the word <u>runner</u>. Rumbling tells what sound Lion makes as he comes to Aardvark's tree. It describes Lion's growl. I don't think it's a happy sound.

(See pages 16–29 for the entire story "Awful Aardvark.")

READING NONFICTION

Nonfiction gives you information about real things. Sometimes nonfiction has pictures and charts. Sometimes headings show the different parts of the story.

It helps to use a strategy to read nonfiction. One strategy is called **K-W-L.** The chart can help before, during, and after your reading.

- **K** stands for "What I **K**now." Preview the story by reading the title and looking at the pictures. Ask yourself what you already know about the topic.

- **W** stands for "What I **W**ant to Know." Think of some questions you want to answer as you read.

- **L** stands for "What I **L**earned." After you have finished reading, think about your questions. Did you get answers? Did you learn what you wanted to? Did you learn anything else?

Mary makes a **K-W-L** chart before she reads "It's an Armadillo!" First, she follows the **K** and **W** steps and writes her ideas and questions on the chart.

K—What I **K**now	**W**—What I **W**ant to Know	**L**—What I **L**earned
lives on land has a head and a body breathes air	What is unusual about the armadillo's body? Where do armadillos live? What do they eat?	

Mary thinks about the **W** questions as she reads.

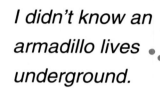

I didn't know an armadillo lives underground.

It's an Armadillo!

by Bianca Lavies

What has left these tracks in the sand? Something with four feet and a tail. You can see its footprints. You can see the groove made by its tail. Where did it go?

It went into its burrow underground. The burrow keeps it cool in summer and warm in winter.

During the day, it sleeps there in a nest. In the evening, it will leave the burrow.

Here it comes. It's an armadillo!

There are several kinds of armadillos in the world. This one is called a nine-banded armadillo. The bands look like stripes around her middle. With her nose and claws, the armadillo roots up leaves and twigs. She is searching for food—beetles, grubs, and ant eggs. Sometimes she also eats berries or juicy roots.

Every now and then the armadillo sits up on her hind legs and listens. She cannot see very well, but she can hear the sounds around her: a leaf rustling, a twig breaking—even a camera clicking.

These bands around the armadillo are interesting.

Here's what the armadillo eats—insects and berries.

After Mary read the story, she thought about what she had learned. Then she wrote what she had learned in the **L** part of the chart. What do you think she wrote?

(See pages 30–41 for the entire story "It's an Armadillo!")

VOCABULARY STRATEGIES

As you read, you will sometimes see words you don't know. When that happens, you can use strategies to help you figure out the words.

When you find a word you don't know, read some more. Do you understand the story without that word? If you do, keep on reading.

What if the story doesn't make sense without that word? Then use these strategies.

- Check the letters at the beginning and the end of the word. What sounds do the letters stand for? Put the sounds together. Does it sound like a word you know?

- Look at the words and the sentences around the word. They are called the **context.** Sometimes they can help you figure out the word you do not know.

- Look for the parts of the word that you know. They may help you figure out the whole word.

- If you can't figure out the word, look it up in a **dictionary** or a **glossary,** or ask your teacher or a classmate.

Read the paragraph about snakes on the next page. You will see how to use strategies to figure out some words you may not know.

Figuring out the sounds may not help if you have not heard the word reptile before. But the next sentence is a **context clue.** It tells you that a snake must be one kind of reptile.

When you check the sounds, you will probably find you know the word poisonous. You can see the word poison in it, and you know that some snakes are poisonous.

The **suffix** -less means "without." So harmless means "without harm."

These three snake names are all **compound words**. Each one is made of two other words. They tell what the snakes are like. A rattlesnake is a snake with rattles in its tail. A copperhead has a head the color of copper metal. A cottonmouth's mouth looks like white cotton inside.

The sentence "Some are even afraid of pictures of snakes" may help you figure out that scared means "afraid."

Many people are scared of snakes. Some are even afraid of pictures of snakes! This is too bad, because these reptiles are interesting to learn about. People should be careful about the poisonous snakes, but most snakes are harmless. Only four kinds of poisonous snakes live in the United States. They are the coral snake, the rattlesnake, the copperhead, and the cottonmouth. The other snakes you might meet in the woods or on a sunny rock won't bother you.

SPEAKING

It is probably easy for you to talk to your friends after school or on the telephone. But it can be hard to talk in front of your whole class. Some strategies can make this easier.

- **Plan** what you are going to say. Are you giving an oral report to your class? Are you talking to your class about a book? Have your ideas in order.

- **Practice** your talk. Listen to yourself. Ask a partner how you can do it better.

Amira and Pedro are reading books about unusual animals. Their teacher wants them to tell a first-grade class about these animals.

Amira plans what she will tell the first graders about the platypus. She will say that it has a bill and lays eggs like a duck. It is furry like a cat. She wants to show a picture of this strange animal, too.

Pedro practices his talk about the armadillo. He wants to make sure he speaks slowly and clearly when he tells about this animal and says its name in Spanish. When he practices, his partner says he can hear all of Pedro's words clearly.

LISTENING

When you listen to people speak, you need to **be quiet.** This strategy will help you listen. Here are some other strategies for listening.

- **Pay attention** to what the speaker says.
- **Set a purpose** for listening, and think about what you will hear. You can listen to learn things. You can listen to get directions. You can listen just for the fun of it!
- **Respond** in the right way to what you hear. Laugh when your friend tells a silly joke but not when she tells about her broken arm. After a speaker is finished, you may want to clap and ask questions.

Here is how the first graders listen to Amira and Pedro.

Amira's audience listens quietly because they have never heard of the <u>platypus</u>. When Amira says that a platypus seems to be made from parts of many animals, the first graders laugh. After Amira finishes, Amy asks where to find a book about a platypus.

The first graders pay attention when Pedro says that the Spanish name <u>armadillo</u> means "little armored one." The audience claps at the end. Some try to say the Spanish name.

THE WRITING PROCESS

The writing process is a strategy for writing better. Follow the steps in the writing process to describe your new kitten to classmates, to write a thank-you letter to your cousin, or to tell your sister how to make pizza.

If you are not happy with what you have done in any step of the writing process, just start again!

Before Matthew begins the steps, he asks himself some questions and decides the answers.

1. **Who** will read my writing?   My classmates will read it.
2. **What** kind of writing will I do?   I will describe something.
3. **Why** am I writing?   I want to make people laugh.

Now Matthew can start the writing process.

PREWRITING

Matthew begins by thinking about a writing idea, or **topic.** He writes down a list of ideas.

1. boa constrictors
2. my favorite dinosaur
3. growing flowers

Matthew looks over his list. He decides he doesn't know enough about boa constrictors. Growing flowers would be a better topic for a how-to paragraph than for a description.

He would like to describe his favorite dinosaur, Allosaurus. But everything he knows is in books. Matthew knows he shouldn't copy what is in a book. So he decides to make up a funny dinosaur to describe.

Matthew thinks up a dinosaur that can play a guitar with its little front legs. Its name is Guitarosaurus. Matthew draws a picture of it. Around it he writes details about the dinosaur.

Guitarosaurus

Looks
Little front legs with guitar
Horns
Colored spots
Spikes on back
Big tail

Sounds
Music
Horns blow—toot
Spikes make a noise
Tail thumps

With his topic and some details clearly in his mind, Matthew is ready to go on to the next step.

DRAFTING

Matthew is ready to write his first draft. Here are some things he does as he writes.

- He starts with an interesting sentence about his topic.
- He uses details from his drawing.
- He just writes his ideas down for now. He doesn't worry about mistakes. He can fix them later.
- He uses words that will make other people "see" and "hear" Guitarosaurus.

> Did you know that their once was a dinosaur called Guitarosaurus? He played a gitar. There were two big horns on his nose. He blue music out of them. He was all covered with colored spots. Theyd go on and off with the music. Lots of metel spikes was down his back. they made a noise when he shook them. He thumped with his big tail. He made toting. thumping music

Matthew reads his draft again. If he doesn't like what he has written, he can write it over. He decides he likes it, so he goes on to the next step.

RESPONDING AND REVISING

Matthew asks some friends to read his draft and tell him how to make it better. Here is what they said.

This is really good! But tell how he plays the guitar.

Instead of _go on and off_, say _blink_.

I like the part about the spikes. I think _rattled_ would be a good word for the sound they make.

Matthew likes their ideas. He sees some other changes he wants to make, too. He uses editor's marks to show them.

EDITOR'S MARKS

∧ Add something.

𝒆 Take out something.

⁀ Change something.

↻ Move something.

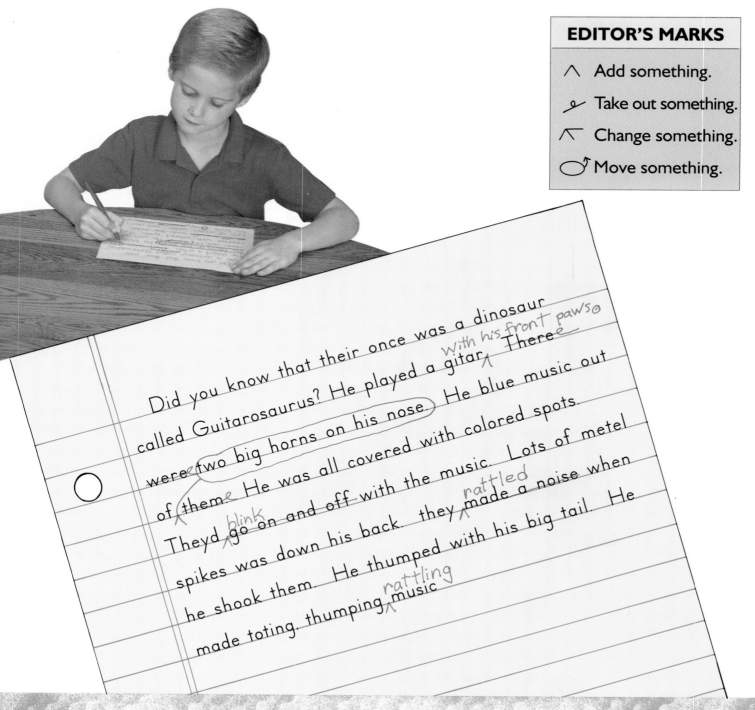

Did you know that their once was a dinosaur called Guitarosaurus? He played a gitar. There were two big horns on his nose. He blue music out of them. He was all covered with colored spots. Theyd go on and off with the music. Lots of metel spikes was down his back. they made a noise when he shook them. He thumped with his big tail. He made toting. thumping music

with his front paws

blink

rattled

rattling

PROOFREADING

Now that Matthew has made his changes, he looks over his paragraph for errors. He uses more editor's marks.

EDITOR'S MARKS	
≡ Use a capital letter.	✄ Take out something.
⊙ Add a period.	⋀ Change something.
⋀ Add something.	◯ Check the spelling.

Matthew circles words that are not spelled right. He writes the correct spelling above them.

Did you know that (their) — *there* — once was a dinosaur called Guitarosaurus? He played a (gitar) — *guitar* — with his front paws. He (blue) — *blew* — music out of two big horns on his nose. He was all covered with colored spots. (Theyd) — *They'd* — blink with the music. Lots of (metel) — *metal* — spikes ~~was~~ *were* down his back. they rattled when he shook them. He thumped with his big tail. He made (toting) — *tooting*, thumping, rattling music⊙

Matthew changes <u>was</u> to <u>were</u> with this mark ⋀.

Matthew should have started the sentence with a capital letter. He underlines the <u>t</u> three times like this ≡.

Matthew forgot the period at the end of this sentence. He adds it like this ⊙.

Matthew is careful when he looks over his spelling. Here are some things he checks.

- He looks for words with two vowels together. He makes sure he has written all the vowels. He adds a <u>u</u> to <u>guitar</u>.

- He looks for words that sound alike but are spelled differently. He changes <u>blue</u> to <u>blew</u> and <u>their</u> to <u>there</u>.

- He checks to see if he has spelled words with apostrophes correctly. He changes <u>Theyd</u> to <u>They'd</u>.

- He looks for words that need double letters. He adds an <u>o</u> to <u>tooting</u>.

- If Matthew can't figure out how to spell a word, he looks it up in the dictionary. He looks up <u>metal</u>.

PUBLISHING

When his corrections are marked, Matthew copies his paragraph in his best handwriting. He makes all the corrections. Now he will publish his description. He can just let his classmates read it or he can do something else.

- He might record his paragraph on a tape. He could ask a friend to help him add sound effects of the Guitarosaurus's music.
- He decides to draw his Guitarosaurus on a white T-shirt with markers that won't wash off. He makes a card and copies his paragraph inside. He sends the shirt and the card to his cousin as a birthday gift.

THE LIBRARY

A library is a place to find books. Two kinds of books are fiction and nonfiction.

Fiction books are stories that were made up by authors. Some stories in this book, such as "Awful Aardvark," are fiction. Some fiction books are about things that could really happen. Some are about things that could never happen.

Fiction books are put on the library bookshelves in ABC order by the author's last name. <u>Awful Aardvark</u> was written by Mwalimu. Look for it on the bookshelves marked with an **M** because **Mwalimu** begins with an **M**.

Nonfiction books are about real people, places, or things. Nonfiction is not made up. <u>It's an Armadillo!</u> is nonfiction because it tells about a real animal.

Nonfiction books are in a different part of the library. Books about the same subject are grouped together. You would find <u>It's an Armadillo!</u> with other books about armadillos.

The librarian will help you find a book, maybe by showing you how to use a computer. Many libraries have all their books listed in a computer.

The librarian can also help you learn to use the **card catalog** to find books. The card catalog is a set of drawers full of cards. The cards have the title and the author of every book in the library written on them. The cards are grouped in ABC order by the first word on the card.

What if you want to find out who wrote the fiction book <u>Awful Aardvark?</u> Look in the drawer marked with an **A**, because <u>Awful</u> is the first word in the title of the book. When you find the card with the title, you will find the author's name.

What if you want to see what books besides <u>It's an Armadillo!</u> Bianca Lavies has written? Look in the **L** drawer for cards that begin with the name Lavies. These cards will have the titles of other books she has written.

title card

> Awful Aardvark.
> J   Mwalimu.
> Mwa Awful Aardvark / Mwalimu ;
>   Illustrated by Adrienne Kennaway.
>   Boston : Little, Brown, c1989

author card

> J   Lavies, Bianca
> 599.31 It's an Armadillo! / Bianca Lavies ;
>   Text and photos by Bianca
>   Lavies.
>   New York : E.P. Dutton, c1989

NOTE TAKING/RESEARCH SKILLS

Nonfiction is writing that gives information about real people, places, and things. When you read nonfiction, you may want to remember some of this information. There are strategies that can help you keep track of what you want to remember.

- Use the strategies for reading nonfiction that you find on pages 280 to 283 in this book.

- Look for the main ideas about each topic. Those are the ones you will probably want to remember. Not everything is important to remember.

- Write down these ideas. Writing down the important points is known as **taking notes.** Make sure that your notes are clear so they will remind you of what you read. You can write your notes on separate pieces of paper or in a notebook. You can make a list or a chart of the facts. You don't have to write whole sentences. Write only the words that will remind you of what you read.

- Using your notes, tell yourself in your own words what you have learned. This is known as **summarizing.**

Here are the notes Rodney took as he began to read this article about sharks.

SHARKS, SHARKS, SHARKS!

Sharks live in oceans all over the world. They are most often found in warm seas.

The biggest shark is the whale shark. It can be 60 feet long and weigh 15 tons. It weighs more than two elephants! The smallest kind of shark is only 4 inches long.

Sharks are different from other fish because they do not have bones. Their skin is rough like sandpaper. The shape of their bodies allows them to swim very quickly. They can swim up to 40 miles per hour. Most sharks will sink if they stop swimming.

A shark's diet is made up of meat. Sharks eat fish and even other sharks. They do not attack people normally. Even so, you should always be careful when you are swimming in the ocean. Stay out of deep water and never swim alone.

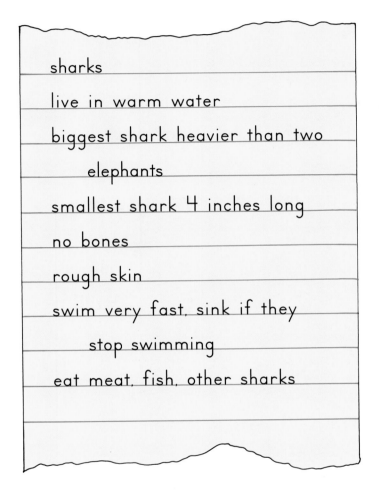

sharks

live in warm water

biggest shark heavier than two

elephants

smallest shark 4 inches long

no bones

rough skin

swim very fast, sink if they

stop swimming

eat meat, fish, other sharks

Rodney tells himself a summary in his own words.

Sharks live in warm water. The biggest shark is heavier than two elephants, and the smallest one is only four inches long. Sharks have rough skin and no bones. They swim very fast and will sink if they stop swimming. Sharks eat meat.

GLOSSARY

The **Glossary** can help you understand what words mean. It gives the meaning of a word as it is used in the story. It also has an example sentence to show how to use the word in a sentence.

The words in the **Glossary** are in ABC order. ABC order is also called **alphabetical order.** To find a word, you must remember the order of the letters of the alphabet.

Suppose you wanted to find *brilliant* in the **Glossary.** First, you find the **B** words. **B** comes near the beginning of the alphabet, so the **B** words must be near the beginning of the **Glossary.** Then, use the guide words at the top of the page to help you find the entry word *brilliant.* It is on page 303.

A **synonym,** or word that has the same meaning, sometimes comes after an example sentence. It is shown as *syn.*

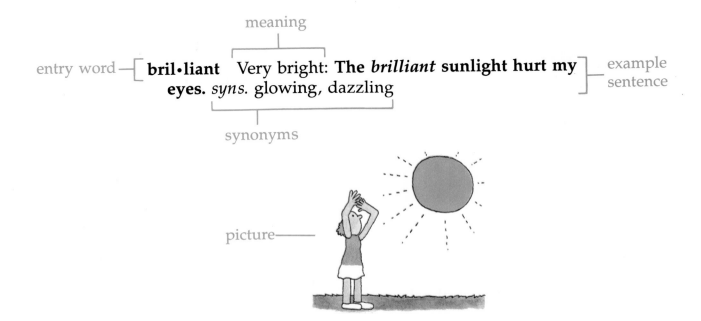

meaning

entry word — **bril·liant** Very bright: **The *brilliant* sunlight hurt my eyes.** *syns.* glowing, dazzling

example sentence

synonyms

picture

A

angry

af·ter·noon   The time of day between morning and evening: **We get out of school in the _afternoon_.**

a·gainst   In the other direction; opposite: **Our team played _against_ theirs last week.**

a·live   Living; not dead: **I was glad to see my bean plant was still _alive_ after I forgot to water it.**

an·gry   Very mad: **I felt very _angry_ when my bicycle got a flat tire.**

an·noy   To make someone mad or unhappy: **Carmen hid my toy to _annoy_ me.** _syn._ bother

an·oth·er   One more: **After I ate one piece of pie, I asked for _another_ piece.**

ar·tist   A person who draws or paints: **The _artist_ painted a picture of Mary's family.**

a·shamed   Upset because you have done something that you think is silly, wrong, or not good enough: **I felt _ashamed_ when I forgot Jim's birthday.** _syn._ embarrassed

a·void   To stay away from: **I walked the other way to _avoid_ stepping into the puddle.**

aw·ful   Very bad: **Marco said the cake tasted so _awful_ he couldn't eat it.**

artist

B

beau·ti·ful   Very pretty; lovely: **It is a _beautiful_ day for a walk in the park.**

bor·ing   Not interesting: **The movie was so _boring_ we fell asleep.** _syn._ dull

brave Having courage; facing danger: **The** *brave* **lifeguard rescued the baby.**

bril·liant Very bright: **The** *brilliant* **sunlight hurt my eyes.** *syns.* glowing, dazzling

brook A small river: **We went fishing in the** *brook*. *syns.* stream, creek

built Made something; put something together: **My grandfather** *built* **the house we live in.**

brilliant

C

caught Trapped; held: **The spider** *caught* **the fly in its web.**

chance A turn to do something: **Maria asked her teacher for a** *chance* **to answer the question.** *syn.* opportunity

change To make or become different: **Minnie decided to** *change* **her drawing by adding a zebra to it.**

choose To pick or select: **I had to** *choose* **between the red and the green lunch box.**

clev·er Smart; good at doing things: **The** *clever* **girl helped the children learn the new game.**

cour·age Bravery when facing something dangerous or when afraid: **Sam showed** *courage* **when he saved the boy from drowning.** *syn.* heroism

built

cov·er To hide or lie on top of: **The falling snow began to** *cover* **the ground.**

co·zy Warm and comfortable: **I sit in my** *cozy* **chair by the fire on winter evenings.** *syn.* snug

cu·ri·ous Very interested to learn or know more: **Cats are so** *curious* **that they seem to want to find out about everything.**

cover

design

de·light·ed Very happy: **I was** *delighted* **to see my old friend.**

de·mand·ed Asked for very strongly: **The worker** *demanded* **that he be paid for his job.** *syn.* insisted

de·sign A pattern of form or color: **The wallpaper's** *design* **is made of purple stripes and orange flowers.**

dis·ap·pear To go away or become hidden: **We watched the plane** *disappear* **into the clouds.** *syn.* vanish

dis·tance A place far away: **I thought I saw Anna waving to me in the** *distance.*

dis·turb To bother or upset: **We hoped the squirrel would not** *disturb* **the bird house and cause the birds to leave.**

dye A liquid used to color cloth: **Kirby soaked the white shirt in purple** *dye* **to change its color.**

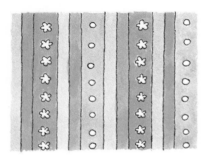

dye

ex·cit·ed Full of feeling: **Tammy is** *excited* **about having a new puppy.**

fa·mil·iar Seen before; well-known: **The girl's face looked** *familiar,* **but Juan couldn't remember her name.**

fam·i·ly A group of people who are related to each other: **There are five people in my** *family.*

fla·vor   The seasoning of food; taste: **I like the** *flavor* **of chocolate.**

fol·low   To come after or behind: **When we march in the parade, my brother will go first and I will** *follow* **him.**

follow

forced   Made someone do something: **The cold** *forced* **me to wear my mittens.**

fu·ri·ous   Very angry: **Jan was** *furious* **when she got the bad news.**

G

guest   A person who is invited to stay or eat with someone else: **Max cooked dinner for his** *guest.*
syn. visitor

H

healthy

harm·ful   Dangerous; able to hurt or cause harm: **Eating junk food is** *harmful* **to your body.**

health·y   Good for someone or something; not sick or weak: **The plant looked green and** *healthy* **after I gave it water.**

I

in·gre·di·ents   Parts of a recipe or mixture: **Flour and sugar are two** *ingredients* **in cookie dough.**

keen   Sharp; very strong: **Dogs have a** *keen* **sense of hearing that allows them to hear things people can't.**

light

larg·er   Bigger: **The balloon got** *larger* **and larger until it popped!**

light   To cause to burn or give off light; to turn on: **Dad used matches to** *light* **the candle.**

light·ning   A sudden flash of light in the sky that happens during a storm: **The** *lightning* **lit up the sky during the storm.**

live·ly   Active; full of life: **The teacher smiled at the** *lively* **children running and shouting on the playground.**

lightning

ma·te·ri·al   Cloth: **Jan bought blue** *material* **to make a dress.** *syn.* fabric

milk   A white liquid food that baby animals get from their mothers' bodies: **Newborn lambs drink their mothers'** *milk.*

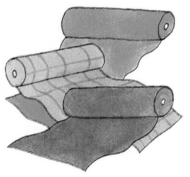

material

once   One time: **I went to the fair only** *once* **last year.**

P

per·suad·ed Talked someone into doing something: **The people *persuaded* the city to build a new park for their children.**

pol·lute To make something dirty: **People *pollute* water by dumping garbage into it.**

pollute

pres·ent A gift; something nice that a person gives someone: **Everyone who came to Jim's party brought him a birthday *present*.**

pro·tect To keep from harm: **I put on mittens to *protect* my hands from the cold.** *syn.* guard

present

R

raise To get or gather together: **We held a bake sale to *raise* money for the school band.** *syn.* collect

reach To stretch out to touch or take something: **I tried to *reach* the apple, but it was too high for me.**

re·ceived Was given; got: **I *received* a bicycle for my birthday.**

rec·i·pe A list of ingredients and directions for making a food: **Please help me find the *recipe* for cornbread.**

reach

re·sourc·es Supplies of things that can be used: **The natural *resources* of the earth include trees, water, and air.**

scene

scissors

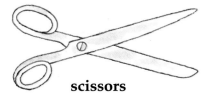

supper

tangled

throwing

S

scene   A picture; a certain place at a certain time: **The postcard showed a *scene* of trees with mountains.** *syn.* view

scis·sors   A tool with two blades used for cutting: **I cut the paper in half with my *scissors*.**

sense   Reasonable meaning: **I like your idea because it makes *sense*.**

spoil   To ruin something so that it can't be used: **You will *spoil* the cake if you add too much salt to the batter.**

stretch·ing   Making longer: **We saw the giraffe *stretching* its neck to eat the leaves on the tree.**

sup·per   Dinner; a meal eaten in the evening: **Our family eats *supper* together every night.**

sup·pose   To imagine or believe that something is true: **I *suppose* you're hungry, since you haven't eaten all day.** *syn.* guess

T

tang·led   Twisted and trapped: **The small butterfly could not escape because it was *tangled* in the net.**

taste   Flavor; what makes food different and special in your mouth: **I love the *taste* of fresh strawberries.**

them·selves   Their own selves: **The children looked at *themselves* in the big mirror.**

thor·ough·ly   Completely; without skipping anything: **Mom told us to clean our rooms *thoroughly*.**

throw·ing   Tossing: **Let's practice *throwing* the baseball.**

tough·er   Stronger; harder: **If you go barefoot on the beach a lot, the bottoms of your feet will get** *tougher* **than they are now.**

trou·ble   Difficulty; problem: **The bike caused Tonia** *trouble* **because the seat kept coming loose.**

tun·nels   Long, narrow spaces dug underground: **The ants dug** *tunnels* **in the ground in our backyard.** *syn.* passages

tunnels

W

weath·er   The way things are outside: **I like the cool, dry** *weather* **in the fall.**

weave   To make cloth by lacing threads over and under each other: **I can** *weave* **potholders on a little loom.**

wool   The thick, soft hair taken from sheep or some kinds of goats and used to make clothing: **I wear sweaters made from** *wool* **when it's cold outside.**

world   The place where we live; the life around us: **We were in our own special** *world* **up in the treehouse.**

weave

Acknowledgments continued

Plays, Inc.: "Stone Soup" by James Buechler from *Dramatized Folk Tales of the World*, edited by Sylvia E. Kamerman. Text copyright © 1971 by Plays, Inc.

Clarkson N. Potter, Inc.: From *How Green Are You?* (Retitled: "Let's Help Save the Earth") by David Bellamy. Text copyright © 1991 by Botanical Enterprises (Publications) Ltd.

Marian Reiner, on behalf of Lilian Moore: "Ants Live Here" from *I Feel the Same Way* by Lilian Moore. Text copyright © 1967 by Lilian Moore.

Scholastic, Inc.: Ibis: A True Whale Story by John Himmelman. Copyright © 1990 by John Himmelman. *Tyrone the Horrible* by Hans Wilhelm. Copyright © 1988 by Hans Wilhelm. Cover illustration by Steve Björkman from *I Hate English!* by Ellen Levine. Illustration copyright © 1989 by Steve Björkman.

Simon & Schuster Books for Young Readers, a division of Simon & Schuster, Inc.: Cover illustration by Sheila Hamanaka from *The Terrible Eek* by Patricia A. Compton. Illustration copyright © 1991 by Sheila Hamanaka. Cover illustration by Armen Kojoyian from *A Drop of Honey* by Djemma Bider. Illustration copyright © 1989 by Armen Kojoyian.

Tambourine Books, a division of William Morrow & Company, Inc.: Cover illustration by James E. Ransome from *How Many Stars in the Sky?* by Lenny Hort. Illustration copyright © 1991 by James E. Ransome.

Handwriting models in this program have been used with permission of the publisher, Zaner-Bloser, Inc., Columbus, Ohio.

Photograph Credits

Key: (t) top, (b) bottom, (l) left, (r) right, (c) center.

11, HBJ/Maria Paraskevas; 12–13(all), HBJ Photo; 14–15, HBJ/Maria Paraskevas; 16, HBJ Photo; 30, HBJ Photo; 31–40(all), Bianca Lavies; 44–45, HBJ/Britt Runion; 46, Gabor Demjen/Aperture, Inc., Boston; 61, HBJ/John Chapnick/Black Star; 78, Courtesy, Bernard Most; 82, HBJ Photo; 96, Harvey Wang/Picture Group; 99, HBJ/Debi Harbin; 100–101(all), HBJ Photo; 104, HBJ Photo; 117, SuperStock; 118–129(all), HBJ/Dale Higgins; 134–135, HBJ/Rich Franco; 148, HBJ/Doug Wilson/Black Star; 149, HBJ Photo; 156, HBJ/Debi Harbin; 184, HBJ Photo; 185(all), Envision; 187(t), 187(b), HBJ/Maria Paraskevas; 188–189(all), HBJ Photo; 190–191, HBJ Photo; 222, HBJ/Doug Wilson/Black Star; 242–243, HBJ/Maria Paraskevas; 244, HBJ/Rich Franco; 270, Tom McCarthy/Transparencies; 275, 276, 277, 279, HBJ/Earl Kogler; 281, 282, 284, HBJ/Britt Runion; 286(l), 286(r), 287(l), 287(r), HBJ/Maria Paraskevas; 288, 291, 292, 294, HBJ/Earl Kogler; 305, Lars Ternblad/The Image Bank.

Illustration Credits

Key: (t) top, (b) bottom, (l) left, (r) right, (c) center.

Table of Contents Art

Tina Holdcroft, 4 (tl), 5 (br), 6–7 (c), 9 (tr); Burton Morris, 5 (tr), 8 (tl), 9 (br); Tim Raglin, 4–5 (bl) (c), 7 (tr), 8 (bl); Peggy Tagel, 6 (l), 7 (br), 8–9 (c).

Unit Opening Patterns

Dan Thoner

Bookshelf Art

Nathan Jarvis, 12–13; Yan Nascimbene, 100–101; Donna Ruff, 188–189.

Theme Opening Art

Roger Chandler, 190–191; Seymour Chwast, 14–15; Peter Horjus, 44–45; Paul Moisel, 156–157; Kirsten Soderland, 102–103; Walter Stuart, 64–65; Jean and Mou-sien Tseng, 64–65; Dale Verzaal, 224–225.

Theme Closing Art

Peter Horjus, 63, 269; Cecelia Laureys, 223; Kenton Nelson, 43, 155, 183; Kirsten Soderland, 131; Walter Stuart, 95; Dale Verzaal, 241.

Connections Art

Gerald McDermott, Lynn Rowe Reed, 184–185, 270–271.

Selection Art

Adrienne Kennaway, 16–29; Shel Silverstein, 42; Steven Kellogg, 47; Olive Jar Productions, 46; Simms Taback, 62; Bernard Most, 66–81; Hans Wilhelm, 82–94; Frané Lessac, 104–116; Carmen Lomas Garza, 118–130; Demi, 134–147; Demi, 150–154; Keith Baker, 158–171; Douglas Gutierrez, Maria Fernandez Oliver, 172–182; Nancy Winslow Parker, 192–202; Charles Schulz, 203; Patricia Polacco, 204–220; Marilyn Hafner, Darrin Johnston, 221; Jennifer Hewitson, 226–227; Arthur Dorros, 228–240; John Himmelman, 244–255; Lynne Cherry, 256–265; Tom Cooke, 266–268.